The Dancing Bears:
Queer Fables for the End Times

Rob Costello

LETHE
PRESS

Typesetting: Ryan Vance

Cover design by Inkspiral Design.

For Werner,
who makes everything possible
and worthwhile.

Contents

"I thought about how stupid it is, that all of us are born destined to desire somebody else, though desire brings with it such disappointment and pain. Humankind's history must be scored bloody with heartbreak. This hankering for affection is a blight upon us."

Sonya Hartnett, *Surrender*

Author's Note

The stories herein represent the work of more than a decade. Many have appeared elsewhere, in various literary, genre, and (even) young adult publications. As written, they were never intended to be gathered like this. Yet, in selecting them for this collection, I was struck by the recurrence of certain themes—obsessions, really—having to do with desire and exploitation, loneliness and despair, fragile masculinity, queer rage, the disillusionment of youth, and a deep-seated anxiety about the state of our world.

In short: my own personal dancing bears.

Make of them of what you will.

Whatever Happened to the Boy Who Fell into the Lake?

Picture Tick at twelve years old, on the day he nearly drowns himself to join Mama.

He's all knees and elbows and goggling green eyes, with fish-belly skin that lobsters in the sun, and greasy black hair that Randall never bothers to make him wash, except if you count all the times he's held Tick's head underwater in the bathtub to teach him to keep his mouth shut about her.

Now, picture a hazy June morning. Declan and Tick by the lake. Declan's blond hair shining like gold in the sunlight, his bronzed skin smelling of soap and grass and black licorice. Tick thinks he's the most beautiful boy in the world, though he hasn't quite figured out what noticing that says about him. He will soon enough.

The two of them stand side by side on the high rocks that look out upon the swimming hole far below. Their toes curl over the edge. They hurl stones into the lake to see who can throw them the farthest. Like all their games of physical prowess, Tick lets Declan win, because holding himself back is the only way he knows how to show love.

He has Mama to thank for that.

Eventually Declan runs out of stones and goes hunting in the woods for more, while Tick hangs around, teetering on the ledge, thinking of her.

He's dreamed of her the night before—he dreams of her most nights—and as he stands in that little corner at the back of nowhere, he pictures once more the imaginary underwater tunnel that, even though he's old enough to know better now, he still secretly hopes is down there at the bottom of the lake, traveling deep beneath the mountains to her new home far out at sea. It's the same silly fantasy he's wished for since he and Randall arrived in Shelter Valley. The one where she swims all the way to the Adirondacks through that tunnel to save him, taking him back with her below the waves to where he belongs: by her side.

By her side, where they'll explore cities of coral with other undersea kids who wear rainbow anemones in their flowing hair. By her side, where she'll introduce him to the lady mermaids who yearn for legs to dance upon the shore. By her side, where he'll climb into her clamshell bed to fall asleep in her arms while she tells him stories of cruel fathers like Randall left far behind on dry land, as friendly sharks swim around to guard them, and no more waking to shouts in the middle of the night, or cigarettes branding the folds of his arms, or fist-shaped bruises recording screams on the secret places beneath his clothes.

He knows he should let go of these childish daydreams, but he can't—he still believes in her. And besides, if there's any magic left in the world, down below must be where it lives. Down where time ebbs and flows with the tides. Where mothers like her ache for the sons they left behind on shore. Yes, he's far too old to cling to such foolish fantasies, but it doesn't matter. The one thing a childhood of secondhand Disney DVDs has taught him is that wishing for something badly enough can sometimes make it come true.

And on this strange, inexplicable morning, it does.

A voice in the wind carries her name to him through the leaves and brambles. When he glances down at his reflection rippling upon the surface of the water, it isn't himself he sees gazing back anymore: It's her.

So, he jumps in after her.

His cries for her are the first thing the lake swallows as it takes him under. His mouth gushes air until no words escape, not even her name. As the green water slithers around him, the undertow coils about his ankles, pulling him down. But he doesn't struggle. He's a stronger boy than Randall gives him credit for being. He wills himself limp, sinking further into the water's keeping. He's daydreamed of joining her in that secret, submerged place for so long. He's wished for it, prayed for it, that beautiful below where sky turns to silver waves and currents refresh like breezes. A world so enchanting and lovely, she chose it over him.

But as he sinks deeper and deeper, thinking, "Mama, I'm here! Mama, I'm ready!" she doesn't come for him. Instead, the darkness presses in. A terrible pain swells in his chest, and his will to hold back crumples beneath the urge to breathe as panic breaks free, jolting him with kicks and spasms. He flails for the surface, grasping at the tendrils of light above. But he's waited too long, gone too deep, and soon nothing remains but the fading pings of his heart as the lake swallows him down ...

He blacks out for whatever happens next.

He doesn't remember anything after that.

He just knows that when they discover him days later and 300 miles away on Rockaway Beach, he is unconscious, naked, and grinning.

But here's the thing: Sometimes magic changes nothing.

Of course, there are news reports when Tick is returned to Shelter Valley. Baffled police. TV cameras. Whispers, rumors, strange looks. Was it an abduction? Did he run away? They say the mother drowned herself on that very same beach. What does the father know? What secrets is that kid hiding anyway?

But eventually these voices grow silent. Such questions don't get answered when folks don't care enough to keep asking them. People lose interest, even the cops. They move on with other business, forget. But they never quite lose their suspicion of Tick.

That boy was never right to begin with—a little too quiet, a little too queer.

Of course, things are different with Randall. Randall knows secrets he's not telling the authorities. Randall hides things from Tick, too. But at least he keeps his hands off his son in the immediate aftermath. There's too much heat, too many eyes on Tick to risk anyone noticing a stray bruise or broken wrist. But Tick knows it's only a matter of time. He knows there are reasons they fled the city after she disappeared. Reasons they moved into this dumpy single-wide at the back end of nowhere, deep in the high, dark mountains.

Tick knows Randall is scared. And when Randall is scared, Tick pays the price.

It's well past midnight six weeks after Tick's return when that bill finally comes due. No knocks. No shouts.

Just the nightmare miasma of Randall's booze breath, while an icy hand covers Tick's mouth. The other hand drags him from the bed by the scruff of his pajamas. The bathroom awaits. Randall's had all evening to prepare, to drink up sufficient rage. He's already filled the grimy tub, its thick rings of skin and scale staining the water an inky black.

"You want me to send you back to her, you ungrateful little fucker?" he says, pushing Tick onto his knees beside the tub. He grabs a thick wad of Tick's hair between his fingers and forces Tick's head over the greasy pool. "'Cause I can do that. I can do it right now."

Then he plunges Tick's face beneath the frigid water.

He holds it there until Tick sees stars.

Tick got used to living with monsters back in the city.

Teeth bared. Eyes red with rage. Fists swinging, feet stumbling, stinking of whiskey and contempt. Tick cowering beneath the sheets as twisted shadows dueled in the yellow light cast on his bedroom wall. The furniture in the living room of the too-tiny Rockaway apartment crashing into bodies. The wind off the Atlantic clawing at his window like a panther scenting blood on the air. It was only when the boys in blue arrived that another night's truce got forged in a haze of cigarettes and raw exhaustion.

What were those fights about? he sometimes wonders. Other men? Other women? It doesn't really matter anymore. Howls and punches were the lullaby of his childhood.

But at least, Tick thinks, she gave as good as she got. Randall still sports the Joker's sneer she carved into the side of his neck that one night with the shattered Old

Crow bottle. A wound that took seventeen stitches to mend. All these years later, and Randall still fingers the scar whenever he tells lies or smokes too much weed. A souvenir of her.

Yes, she gave as good as she got.

Until she was gone.

Sometimes Tick wants to give as good as she gave. On certain battered and bruised nights, as he shakes the water from his ears or holds a towel of ice to a fresh welt, it's all he can do, after Randall passes out in front of the TV, to keep from bashing the old man's brains in with a ball peen hammer or the clothes iron.

Or to burn out his eyes with one of his own cigarettes.

Or to carve another Joker's sneer deep into his windpipe.

On nights like that, Tick knows that he comes from monster's blood.

He wonders sometimes if that's why she left him behind.

If that's why she sent him back here.

It's Declan who listens to all of Tick's half-baked theories about what really happened at the swimming hole that day. Declan who knows the true story of what happened that last time on Rockaway Beach. Declan who cares enough to believe in Tick, despite how crazy it all must sound. Declan who finally suggests another way to find her.

School has begun again. They're on a field trip to the Kayoga County Library when Declan realizes that Tick's stories remind him of a particular fairy tale gone wrong. He can't remember which tale exactly, but maybe he heard it, or read it, or saw it once in some movie.

Maybe Tick can track it down in a library book?

Tick takes his friend's advice to heart and begins the hunt in earnest. But the library has so many books. Books of folklore and fantasy. Storybooks and fairy tales. He hears her echo in the whispering leaves of a juniper tree. He tastes her bitterness in the poisoned apples proffered by sinister hags. He aches for her loss in the wishes granted by fairy godmothers. But these are mere shadows of her, shelf upon shelf, row after row, each neatly bound within the quiet, fervent intimacy of pages. So many shadows, he fears he won't find the real her before it's time to go back to school.

In the end, it's Declan who makes the discovery. In the Myths and Legends section on the second floor. She's in a book called *Tales of the Northern Islands* by Dorothy Shales Green. Her story is a queer one. A sad story. An angry one. A story unlike any of the others because it makes Tick feel something he's never felt before: the shock of recognition.

Declan helps him steal the book just before the teacher gathers them back on the bus.

Tick hides it beneath his mattress at home for safekeeping.

He never returns to the library after that.

It's well after midnight when Tick slips into the black water.

Lately, he's been sneaking down to the swimming hole on moonlit nights like this to think on his own. Though it's a risk that Randall could wake up and find him gone, the lake's the only place he feels safe anymore. The only place he finds solace. Only Declan knows about these late-night swims, though he thinks Tick should stay away from the water after everything that's happened. But the sea was Tick's home long before these mountains.

He knows that now. Whatever happened that day at the swimming hole has awakened that part of her that's still alive in his blood, and this dark little lake is as close as he can get here to feeding it.

Though it's been a sweltering Indian summer, the water is frigid tonight. Still, it's nothing like the bone-gnawing cold of the Atlantic, which he remembers from those long-ago nights when she'd carry him out into the deeper water. How old was he back then? No more than three or four. She'd say, "Don't be afraid, Patrick," as she hoisted him into her arms and walked from the velvety sand into the moonlit surf. Not that he knew enough to be afraid. Though the icy waves sucked at his arms and legs, the saltwater biting his lips and eyes, his innocence made him brave. His trust in her made him forget the peril, and besides, the smell of it, the roar of it, the raw power of it were too exhilarating for fear.

Or at least that's how he remembers it now, though he knows better than to trust these memories implicitly. It's so hard to pull the threads of truth from the crazy quilt of dreams and wishes stitched together in his brain. Yet, when he closes his eyes and floats onto his back to drift on the placid mountain waves, those distinctions slowly blur into abstraction ...

"We come from the sea," she tells him as a planet's worth of ocean courses hungrily around his small, wriggling body. "One day we all return to it."

Her fingers are hot and unyielding clamped around his slender chest as she thrusts him into the onrushing tide like an offering.

"We are together," she assures him above the roar. "Don't be afraid."

But he is not afraid. His desire for the sea is too overpowering, like an instinct, seductive and fierce. He kicks and squirms to be let loose, the yearning inside his frail little heart stronger than fear or self-preservation. He wants to be set free. Though he doesn't have the words to describe this craving, there is an urgent hunger inside him to feel his own essence flowing out into this vast, unfathomable abyss, pure of water and life, of teeming oblivion, until there is nothing left of him, not even his own awareness.

Nothing left but the sheltering sea …

But alas, this is only Shelter Lake.

He gasps and spits out its loamy water, having slipped beneath the surface for too long. As he flounders his way back to shore, he wishes he understood why she didn't let go of him that night or one of the others. Why she waited until later on to let him go.

Why she finally returned for him after all this time, only to send him back here alone.

Here is the tale from that stolen book, pages 187-188:

Once upon a time, a troublesome fisherman was walking off a night of heavy drink on the beach when he spied three beautiful Selkie maidens dancing nude in the surf. Beside them lay their discarded sealskins stretched out across the rocks to dry in the first rays of dawn.

The fisherman could not at first believe his own lustful eyes, for each of these maidens was more beautiful than the last. He resolved then and there that he would have one of them for his own, and thus, while they frolicked heedlessly in the waves, he stole up behind the rocks and snatched one of their sealskins, retreating to a nearby cave where he hid it in a place it would not be found. Then he waited for the right moment to claim his prize.

This arrived some hours later when, upon returning to the beach, he found the most beautiful of the three maidens squatting upon the sand, crying bitterly over the loss of her sealskin.

The fisherman, though low of character and cruel of heart, was also handsome and charming. With false promises of aid and shelter, he managed to coax the frightened Selkie back to his cabin, where he barred the door and forced his way upon her.

Yet as soon as he'd finished the terrible deed, a queer and powerful fatigue overwhelmed him. He fell immediately into a troubled sleep filled with nightmares of drowning in storm-tossed seas. When he awoke sometime later, the Selkie loomed over him, the sharp blade of a filet knife pressed firmly to his throat.

"I would kill you where you lie for what you have done to me," she said, her eyes ablaze with hatred. "But you have filled me with your child. By the custom of my folk, I am bound to you until that child is born. But please understand: From this day forth you are cursed. Everything you touch will crumble. Every scheme you hatch will fail. All that you love will wither and die. Each day of our lives together will be a misery, and our poor child must bear this fate as well. This is the price you and your offspring shall pay for what you have done to me, for I will not be tamed by any man."

And sure enough, the Selkie's curse came true.

The fisherman's love of drink soon became his bane and ruination. His nets returned empty while those of others yielded bounties of slippery silver fish. His moods darkened, turning him vicious and cruel. His handsome features twisted into a haggard leer, and he beat the pregnant Selkie night after night without mercy.

But she never broke, and she never wept.

Thus was the home into which their cursed child—a slippery, mewling boy—was born and grew. A home of strife and violence and sadness. A home of sullen days and stormy nights. The lad's father could not stand the sight of him, and though he was loved in a fashion by the Selkie, it was a sick and resentful love, tainted by bitterness and shame.

Yet the work of the curse was not done, for even the fisherman's original scheme to entrap the Selkie maiden would, some five years later, finally crumble to dust.

On that day, while playing in a cave by the cliffs, the young lad discovered his mother's hidden sealskin where it should never have been found. He ran home to present her with this strange trophy, hoping to please her, and to his delight it did.

But the lad's happiness proved short-lived, for he awoke from a troubled sleep before dawn the next morning to find his mother gone. Stricken with a foreboding he did not comprehend, he raced down to the beach in time to watch as the Selkie, draped from head to toe in her recovered sealskin, walked straight into the onrushing tide. There she transformed back into her true, wild self, vanishing beneath the waves forever, without so much as a backward glance at the brokenhearted son she left behind.

Tick knows winter is always on its way in these mountains.

Summer's warmth and light are the exceptions that prove the stark rules of endurance here. Families begin cutting their firewood for next season as soon as the snow melts. The county road crews work fourteen-hour days from May to September to repair all the potholes that cleave open again by Christmas. Cardigans and afghans never leave the backs of chairs, and fleeces, boots, and mittens haunt every closet, biding their time for resurrection.

They won't have much longer to wait.

When Tick and Declan walk home from the school bus stop one late September afternoon, he can see his breath on the air for the first time since spring. The leaves are blushing. Soon they'll drop, and then the snow and darkness will rush in.

Autumn has barely begun, and he's already dreading what lies ahead.

Tick hates Shelter Valley winters. The cold seeps into his bones and hardens there like wax as the days begin to feel like sifting through the ashes of hope for smaller and smaller nuggets to burn. At school, he watches the light drain from his teachers' eyes as the landscape outside sharpens into juts of gray and white.

But the worst part is getting trapped at home with Randall. The endless dark and unyielding cold stoke his father's resentments like a furnace, choking Tick on the fumes. When Randall leans hard into his grievances it burns blazing hot. By March, when there's no money left for heating oil, and they're eating mayonnaise sandwiches through chattering teeth, the old man is incandescent to be around. Any spark will light his fuse.

But at least there's Declan.

Declan, who's taken to holding Tick's hand when nobody else is around.

Declan, whose first kiss tastes of the honeyed warmth of a high summer breeze.

Declan, whose smile shines like the sunrise cutting through Tick's stormy gray night.

Declan is a boy who will always be loved.

He is the light that Tick is not.

*

The dream Tick describes to Declan is always the same:

He's a mouse scurrying behind her as she scuttles down the back stairs and out into the bitter March air. Seagulls squeal overhead, gliding across a gunmetal sky. The other houses on the street are dark. Dawn isn't even a promise yet, and as the wind off the Atlantic howls up from the beach, it scorches Tick's face with droplets of saltwater and grains of sand.

She's a tall, dark shape charging toward the boardwalk as he struggles to keep up with her. Although he's shivering in the parka and mittens she stuffed him into when she dragged him out of bed, she doesn't appear to notice the cold herself, wearing the long fur coat he found tucked beneath the floorboards in the attic. The coat's so heavy it weighs her down, bowing her shoulders, borne like a burden. Yet the fur itself is so shimmery and sleek it reminds him of an animal, something fast and vicious that would bite his hand if he tried to pet it.

When she finally comes to a halt at the vacated boardwalk, he scampers up beside her, and together they peer out at the derelict strand. There's nobody around, not even the foolhardy surfers who tempt fate in the wee hours with their flimsy boards and wetsuits. The sea is a tumult of late-winter breakers and spray. The air reeks of ozone and rot. Last night's storm has trashed the beach, belching up a litter of dead fish, beer cans, and seaweed that stretches for miles in either direction. The distant lights of a freighter glisten along the horizon until they dip below the roiling waves and vanish into darkness.

But something about this scene feels wrong. It's unlike all the other nights she's brought him out here in the dark. The thrill and exhilaration are missing. Instead, there is only fear and confusion, the unspoken weight of her sadness.

He grabs her hand, pleads with her to return home, but she wrenches free and shoves him onto a nearby bench with such force he squeals. She doesn't seem to notice how deeply she's frightened him. She's too caught up, too distracted, and though he has no idea why, he knows better than to cry or fuss when this dark mood comes over her. So, he holds back his tears, too afraid to speak or even to look her in the eyes.

But it's already too late.

She turns her back to him then and faces the water, kicks out of her shoes, reaches up to unfasten the fist-shaped bun at the base of her skull. She shakes out her long black hair, letting it cascade freely in the wind. Where it brushes against her shoulders it vanishes into the inky black mass of the coat, almost as if they're made of the same thing. Then she commands him to, "Stay, Patrick," and walks calmly toward the steps that descend to the beach.

The sinking quality of her voice alarms him. There's something wrong about this, something wrong about her. Something more wrong than usual. It's then that he realizes she's letting go of him, and even if those aren't the exact words that form in his preschooler's brain, he's not stupid: He knows how it feels to get left behind.

But she's already far out on the beach by then, the wet sand sucking at her bare feet. Soon, it's replaced by the sizzling surf, her hair whipped into a frenzy until she pulls up the coat's hood to shield her head from the wind.

Tick wants to run after her, but he can't seem to move. He wants to speak, but he doesn't know what to say. All he can do is sit and watch numbly as she strides into the Atlantic, arms outstretched to embrace it. And maybe it's the wind or a trick of the light. Or maybe it's that he's only a little boy and completely terrified. But when the waves reach the level of her chest, it appears to him as if the coat begins to ripple and surge around her body, almost as if it's pulling her into the water. Almost as if it is the water.

That's when he finally finds his voice and cries, "Mama!"

She glances back at him. She does. But she's nothing now but a black shape silhouetted against a black horizon. He can't see the contours of her face shaded beneath the enveloping hood. There's no way to tell if her eyes are reaching out to say goodbye to him, or if they've already vanished into her own private darkness. And when she turns back to face that hungry sea again, a giant swell gapes open and swallows her, whole and forever.

Tick has reached the age of letting go of magic when the first snow of the season falls.

This is the evening he turns thirteen.

The night Randall finds the library book hidden beneath his mattress.

It's well after sunset when Tick trudges home from the little birthday party Declan has asked his mother to throw for him. The snow is already deep, piling in feathery drifts up to his knees. The trailer sits dark, save for the blue light of the TV flickering in the living room window. Randall waits for him inside, on the couch, a nearly empty bottle of Old Crow on the coffee table before him. He's prepared himself for what's to come. The book is spread open in his lap, turned to the pages Tick has marked up with handwriting.

His notes and theories. His accusations. His unanswered questions.

Neither of them speaks. The look on Randall's face conveys all that needs to be said. This is the end of the road for father and son. Her curse has followed them all the way up to the mountains, where Randall foolishly thought he could escape it. But he can no longer pretend that what happened at the swimming hole was a fluke, a one-off, that he can beat and burn and drown her influence out of the boy. Now that Tick knows the truth, Randall can no longer deny that his son is her curse embodied on dry land. Tick is the secret tunnel that will always lead back to her. He is a chain affixing Randall to her anchor, and there's only one way to sever that link.

There will be no punches tonight.

No cigarettes or screams.

The bathtub is already full and waiting, the silent water stained as dark as an open grave.

Tick doesn't put up a fight.

Let this happen, he thinks, as the blackness swallows him. Let it be done quickly. Let it all end here. This curse of being her son. The curse of being abandoned. The curse of this monster's blood. Randall's fists clamp to the back of Tick's neck like an iron brace pulled hot from the forge. The feverish weight of him is implacable as he holds the boy's head underwater. Soon, stars appear in the dark field before Tick's eyes as the pain swells in his slender chest, ready to burst him open, to explode him into teeming oblivion.

But then one of those stars resolves into the sunrise.

Declan.

He will not give up on Declan.

The thought of his friend yields a reckoning. Rage breaks free inside of Tick, jolting him alive with kicks and spasms. He flails for air, gasping at the slippery tendrils of Declan's dying light. He bucks and writhes, grappling to slip free of the powerful man who has him pinioned to the edge of the bathtub, and though for anyone else it would already be too late, already too long without oxygen, Tick is her son:

The water belongs to him.

Suddenly the pings of his heart surge into a roar as all the strength of the mighty Atlantic surges up through whatever unseen tunnel lurks inside him. The sheer force of it overwhelms him, driving him back, shuddering the trailer, rocking the ground beneath it like an earthquake.

Tick blacks out for whatever happens next.

But when he comes to, Randall is lying face down in the bottom of the empty bathtub, his head twisted at an impossible angle, his eyes bulging lividly, a trail of brackish bile oozing from his ruined mouth.

Not knowing what else to do, Tick calls Declan for help.

But when the boy he loves arrives and sees what Tick has done, it's as if all the fullness of winter crashes down upon them. The warmth drains from Declan's face; the summer light winks out of his eyes. A chill rises between the two boys as sharp as blades.

Declan's not listening to Tick's crazy explanations this time.

He doesn't care enough to believe anymore.

He just wants to go home …

Now. *Please.*

Declan backs out of the bathroom, stumbles toward the front door, his fists raised before him, ready to fight for his life.

Tick is stricken. He doesn't know what to do or say. He can see that Declan is terrified of him now, and the shame and horror of this realization are so withering he doesn't even try to stop the boy from running home to his mother.

Instead, Tick just stands there over Randall's corpse as his own heart crumbles to dust.

*

Tick has nowhere else to go but the swimming hole.

The storm has ended, clearing the sky for a fat, fulgent moon. He trudges onward, listless and alone through heavy accumulations of ice and snow, only to discover when he arrives that her curse has not died with Randall:

The lake is frozen over, his only chance for escape cut off.

Tick hurls himself onto the ice, pounding futilely on its impregnable surface, his salty tears refusing to freeze to his cheeks.

"Mama, please," he begs. "Mama, help me!"

But she is not there, she does not come for him, until …

A pinprick of light appears between his knees. It shines like a beacon through the inky depths beneath the ice, growing wider and brighter as an underwater tunnel irises open onto a vast and beautiful below. Soon, he sees a sky of silvery waves yawning widely beneath him. He sees mermaids dancing among the sharks in rainbow cities of coral. He sees an unfathomable abyss, pure of water and life, his own sheltering sea.

All that he's wished for. All that he's wanted.

And yet, it might as well be a dream just beyond his reach on the underside of this frozen floor of ice that remains as unbreakable and unyielding as her.

It isn't until he notices her watching him, silent and cold, that he realizes the bitter truth:

She never left him at all.

She's been with him this whole time, alive and teeming in his monster's blood since that night on the beach when she walked into the surf without saying goodbye.

She's been waiting. Just waiting.

No, Mama never let go of him after all.

Not until now, not until this moment.

Not until his work was done.

That's when the light begins to fade.

That's when the tunnel draws closed behind her.

Soon, there's nothing left to see beneath the ice but her face shining in the moonlight. She smiles sadly at her son, waves him a last goodbye, then turns to vanish into her black forever.

And when they finally come for Tick sometime later, it's Declan who's pointing the way.

I Am the Other One

Two brothers ran through the woods. One me. One you.

Two brothers ran, inhaling August air so thick it clung to our summer-bronzed limbs like a second skin, our shouts and laughter the only sounds that echoed off the mute hearts of the trees that surrounded us.

Two brothers ran, dodging limbs and branches, leaping the swollen roots of hemlock and century oak, scurrying through the brush and darkening green like frenzied rabbits, like kill-hungry hounds.

"Ahh eee!" you called from behind me.

I turned to see you pound your slim, bare chest as if you were the master of our jungle.

You inhaled the moss-rich air and shouted again, "Ahh eee! Ahh eee!"

You were a ripe, blonde-headed boy, built from juts and angles, eyes the green of pond water, strong and tall for your age, yet so frail and vulnerable when matched against the towering world that surrounded us.

Even so, you were more than a match for me.

"Kill the pig!" you cried. "Cut his throat! Kill the pig! Bash him in!"

"Time out!" I skidded to a halt and whirled around to glare at you. "I'm not Piggy! I'm not!" The red-raw sky gaped like an open wound through the trees as I pitched forward, sneakers toeing the loam, hands on knees, heaving and cursing you under my breath. In the distance, a dog bayed in sympathy with my indignation. "I said ... I wouldn't ... be Piggy," I heaved breathlessly. "I meant it."

Unheeding, you leapt buck-like over the brush, your arms outstretched to tag me out.

"I got you," you announced and collapsed against the shining white bark of a birch, sliding down into a ball of breathless titters at my feet.

"But I called time out!" I struggled to frame the injustice of it all. "I told you I wouldn't be Piggy. It's not fair." I had the good sense to turn away to hide my frustrated tears. "We're not playing this stupid game anymore. I won't play it."

You fixed me in a hard glare and pulled yourself to your feet. I braced for the shove that would lead to a scuffle that would end with me toppled onto the ground. But no shove came. Instead, you merely snorted at me. I was not even worth your trouble, although I still watched you warily, waiting. Your face was flush with exertion, your chest surging from your glorious run through the woods. You produced a handkerchief from the pocket of your cutoffs, spit on a cleanish corner, and daubed at a red, wet gash that snaked across your shoulder. Then you flashed me a private smirk and said, almost to yourself, "That's okay. Piggy was a sore loser, too."

"I called time out, you cheater. I hate yo—"

But before I could finish, you were on top of me, all rapid-fire arms and legs. You pushed me to the ground, your ropey thighs pinioning my legs, my arms twisted behind my back, my face shoved into the dirt.

"Ahh eee!" you cried from atop the mound of my writhing body. "Take your punishment like a man, Piggy!"

You leveraged your greater weight to keep me immobile. Although I struggled, you had me trapped. I was the younger one, the weaker one, the one who still cried at night missing Mama. The one who wet the bed. I was at your mercy as you pinned my wrists with one hand and jammed the other down the back of my cutoffs, gathering a handful of damp elastic that you yanked upward with all your might.

I hollered, first with shock, then with rage. But then the taut fabric of my underpants cut into my soft, unripened boy parts and I began to whimper. Without mercy, you pulled harder, harder, until, with a tear so violent I thought an organ had burst inside me, the cotton gave way, rending along the seam. Then you leapt to your feet laughing at me.

I flipped onto my back and sat up, tears streaming down my dusty cheeks.

The baying dog in the distance let out a low, sustained howl, as if scenting our scuffle like the fetor of a cock fight.

You leaned forward and offered me a hand up, but I pushed it away.

"You tricked me," I said, sniffling back my tears.

"You're not Piggy," you said indulgently and then smiled. "But you still lost."

Fuck you and your pity. That's what I would've said if I'd had those words within me back then. But since I didn't, I snorted back my tears and snot, and with all the bile I could muster, I hocked a loogie into your face.

You didn't even flinch, just snagged the handkerchief from where you dropped it and wiped my spittle from your chin. "That was a wormy thing to do," you said quietly. "Be a man if you don't want to be a pig."

Then you strode past me toward the clearing as if stepping over a pile of dog crap.

My rage deflated, and I scrambled to my feet. The flapping elastic of my favorite Justice League Underoos overhung the waist of my cutoffs like the bottom lip of an orangutan. I yanked fitfully at my backside, trying without success to dislodge my violated underpants from all the uncomfortable corners they'd dug themselves into. But after several moments of no luck, I kicked out of the cutoffs, shimmied out of the ruined briefs, and hurled them into the low-hanging branches. Then I slipped back into my shorts and stumbled after you.

By now, the pinks and reds had drained from the evening sky, replaced by the cooler blush of purple-violet flecked with starlight. You stood a few paces ahead in an open pasture of swaying sweetgrass, your arms outstretched, the tallest of the feathery tips brushing the palms of your hands.

"Feeling better?" you asked, not turning to look at me.

Though I took my place behind you, I didn't respond. I couldn't bring myself to apologize.

"I think the old man's gone," you said and gestured to the darkened farmhouse, hunched and brooding on the far side of the pasture. Then you pointed to the chain link kennel backed up against the side of the house. "Corporal's in the pen."

Inside it, I could just make out the black shape of the patrolling Rottweiler.

"What if he gets out?" I asked, suddenly afraid.

It was as if the dog's ears pricked at being discussed, because he let out another low howl.

"Don't be stupid. If he could get out, do you think we'd be standing here now?"

"Don't call me stupid."

I gave you a halfhearted shove.

"Stop it. We don't have time." You turned to look at me, but all I could see was your shadow in the gloaming. "The old man's always back by ten at the latest, but he could show up any minute. The orchard's on the far side of the house, and we still have to get the baskets off the porch." You jerked your head toward the low-slung shoulders of Connecticut Hill on the horizon. "Gramps said the moon rises early tonight. We should meet back here when it does. Whoever has the most peaches wins. Got it?"

"Yeah, I got it—boss."

This was your plan, and like all of your plans I didn't get any say in its execution. What was worse, I knew as sure as the sun would rise that your basket would close out the night holding three times as many peaches as mine. There wouldn't be a competition. That was how it always worked between us. While I lazed away the summer buried in some book, you were off scoping out Old Man Hazzard's orchard, lurking among the trees, observing his routines, fixating on the prize with such a tangible fervor that by the time you came home for dinner, I could practically smell the sweet tang of peaches already on your breath.

Looking back, it was a pointless game. Peaches? We had our own stupid peach tree in the backyard, and Grandma would have bought us bushels more if we'd asked. But what did any of that matter to you? You were poised for victory, and that's all that ever mattered.

Winning. Beating me.

By then you'd already begun to walk toward the house, and after a moment's hesitation, I followed. The pasture was broader than a football field, the ground soft and wet. It sucked at the soles of my sneakers, slowing me down, though you managed to glide effortlessly through the grass to quickly pull ahead of me. You'd just begun to whistle an old Civil War tune from a black and white movie we'd watched with Gramps on TV, when you were suddenly drowned out by an ungodly rush coming from the woods behind me. I spun around to see the great dark cloud emerge from the treetops, a susurration of wings followed by squeals and clicks as the swarm of bats descended upon the ripe mosquito fields of Old Man Hazzard's lower acreage.

And then it was upon you.

Dozens of them spiraling in at you, whirling and cheeping, until you nearly vanished within the funneling vortex of fluttering black bodies. I dropped to my knees and covered my ears against the clamor, but you—*you didn't even flinch*. Instead, as I looked on in horror, you lifted your arms above your head and with a kind of manic glee began to wiggle your fingertips at the heart of the swarm, almost as if to tickle the creatures' underbellies.

"Stop it!" I screamed. "Stop!"

And then it was over.

Corporal let out a mournful howl as the bats veered off, resuming their course to dinner, and then you were looming above me, a shadowy hand outstretched.

"They're gone," you said, and added as if remarking on a minor stunt in a movie, "That was cool."

But I didn't move. I didn't speak. What could I say? It wasn't as if I were surprised. I knew well your uncanny gift. Grandpa called it your "Dolittle." Your ability to commune with the creatures of the wild. Sense their minds. Share their thoughts. Feel their feelings. Though our cows and chickens and goats all ignored you, I'd personally witnessed you run with the whitetail foals as if you were among them. I'd watched you shimmy with the squirrels up the throat of a copper beech taller than the church steeple. I'd seen ravens eat berries out of the palm of your hand, observed a mama lynx curl up in your lap with her newborn kittens, and even gawped dumbfounded while you wrestled with a wild boar as if you were the best of friends. And after each of these episodes, and countless others like them, I'd always felt squeezed inside by the same dread envy that you were different, *special*.

That I could never be like you.

That I would never *be* you.

"One of a kind," Gramps would boast as he tousled your golden hair, and each time he did so, I felt something stir in that small, black chamber of my heart.

I clambered to my feet, refusing your hand.

"Are you ready?" you asked.

"Sure."

But the only thing I was ready to do was to turn around and run home. I wanted to concede defeat, get it over with quickly and painlessly. I wanted to slink back to the book I'd been reading, where at least I might lose myself for an hour or an evening imagining that I could somehow be special, too.

But there was no way I could turn back now.

"Are you sure you want to go through with this?" you said, almost as if you could Dolittle me, my hesitation. I felt you peer at me through the darkness, judging me the way Gramps eyed the evening sky, gauging the color of the clouds for bad weather on the rise. "It'll be okay," you added, not unkindly. "Why don't you just wait here for me?"

Fuck your pity. If only I'd had those words back then. No need to console poor Piggy. But instead, I muttered, "Let's just go," and bolted for the house before you could say another word.

As I ran, the pasture flickered to life around me. Masses of fireflies winked on the air like stardust. The grass swatted my bare skin as the hulking silhouette of the farmhouse loomed ahead, blotting out a larger and larger slice of sky.

Yet, before I'd reached the back porch, my footfalls provoked Corporal into a snarling rage. The chain link clattered tenuously as the dog clawed at his frail enclosure.

I shuddered, slowed, and then stopped, all my nerve dribbling into the dirt at my feet.

"Just ignore him," you called. "He can't get out."

Then you jogged around me.

I watched paralyzed as your shape dashed through the final paces of grass and scuttled up the creaking steps of the back porch. I tried to will myself to follow you, but it was as if my feet had taken root. Corporal howled at our intrusion upon his turf, the chain link groaning and rattling as he hurled himself madly against it.

But nothing happened.

Even so, when you called my name from the porch, I couldn't summon the breath to respond. I was frozen in place by the absolute certainty that I could not take another step.

That is, until you shouted, "Come on, Piggy!"

All at once my toes curled inside my sneakers, uprooting me. I somehow lifted one foot after the other until I was there, tottering at the top of the porch steps beside you.

I said nothing about the insult, too wary to open my mouth so near to the angry dog. Instead, I scanned the porch. It was dimly lit by a lamp somewhere within the house shining through an open window. Corporal's kennel sat not fifteen feet to the left, wedged between the foundation and the end of the porch. I couldn't see the dog inside it, but I could hear him, seething at this inexcusable invasion of his master's domain. I could smell him, too, smell the fetid stink of his unwashed fur and the musk of freshly upturned soil.

"He's trying to dig out," I said urgently.

"Relax," you replied, barely audible over the dog's outbursts as you leisurely rifled through a heap of basket-shaped objects piled beside an old recliner. "Once, I watched a fox take a nap across from that kennel. He never got out, and he was way more worked up than now."

You turned to me, handing over a small wicker basket. It was the kind of dainty thing Grandma might have used to pick blueberries, but I took it anyway, too uneasy to protest.

"Hazzard knew what he was doing when he built that pen," you continued. "There's no way for him to get out unless the old man wants him to. See that?" You gestured at the shape of what appeared to be an overturned question mark dangling in mid-air above the arm of the recliner. It took my brain a moment to resolve it into what it actually was—the curved brass handle of an old cane affixed to a length of rope that hung from the eaves of the porch. "He's got the rope strung to the gate latch, and he's got the gate spring-loaded. One pull on that and it's all over." Disgust crept into your voice as you added, "If the old bastard had been home that day, that fox wouldn't have stood a chance."

You strode across the porch and leaned over the railing beside Corporal's pen. "You're not so tough in there now, are you?"

Corporal leapt and snarled trying to clamber up the side of the pen, but it was no use. The fence was too high.

"Aww, look at the little puppy," you said, your voice syrupy and mocking. "What's the little puppy gonna do?"

"Stop it," I said angrily. I knew you hated that dog. You hated and feared all the creatures you couldn't reach. The domesticated ones, the ones too complacent or trained or skittish to Dolittle with you. Like the colt that threw Mama. But your hate turned you ugly, cruel. Corporal was already too riled up: I was afraid he might hurt himself trying to get out. "He's just a stupid dog. You don't need to be such a bully."

"I'm a bully?" You whirled on me. "You haven't seen him kill anything yet."

You let that sink in for a moment before returning to the pile of baskets.

I didn't know what else to do, so I just stood there watching as you rummaged through the remaining baskets until you'd found the one you wanted. It was at least three times larger than the one you'd handed to me, with a deep belly of woven rushes and a wooden handle as thick as my wrist.

I felt the burn rise to my cheeks. "I'll take one like that," I said, grabbing for it.

"Naw, that's okay." You hoisted it out of my reach. "That one's a better fit."

"But—"

"Come on." You slipped past me and skipped down the steps. "There's no time to argue." Then you disappeared around the corner of the house.

But I didn't follow. Instead, I cursed the worst word I knew how to curse—"Shithead!"—and hurled the little Grandma basket down the length of the porch, where it bounced off the top of the railing and pitched itself into Corporal's kennel. The dog went silent for a moment, startled by the crash, until, with a sudden rush of muscle and fury he pounced upon the invader.

I listened with cold satisfaction to the sound of wood and wicker being torn to shreds, and then I stepped over to the scattered heap of baskets. You'd been sloppy about making your selections. What had been a stack of baskets neatly nested one into the other was now a jumble. I got down on my knees and began to rummage through them, though soon enough I realized there were none as tiny as the one you'd given to me. The runt of the litter.

"Shithead," I cursed again, my blood pounding in my ears. I sucked down a spiteful breath and continued searching for a basket to match the one you'd taken for yourself. But there weren't any others that size, and I was finally forced to settle for one almost as large. Unlike your basket, this one was rectangular and constructed from thin strips of interwoven wood. It had two rusty handles bolted to its sides and reeked of mildew.

It was also ridiculously heavy.

I heaved it into my arms and quickly realized that it would be impossible for me to carry such a bulky thing through the orchard, especially once it was filled with a bounty of ripe peaches. Reluctantly, I set it back down and began to search for a more manageable basket. But they were all the same: too large or heavy or awkwardly configured for my small hands and skinny body to carry, especially when bearing a full load of swollen fruit.

My heart sank.

You'd chosen the right one for me all along.

My arms and legs turned to pillows; I was stuffed with feathers.

What was the point? What was the point?

I stumbled backwards and fell into Old Man Hazzard's recliner. The stench of dust and sweat wafted up from the dirty fabric, but I barely noticed. Corporal's barking had become an enervating drone, like the angry whir of an overheating engine. I rested my head against the cushion and shut my eyes. I drifted back and back, falling further into the gloom behind my eyelids until my mind slipped free of my body, and I could sense it again, that ugly black thing taking shape within me. It sniffed at the corners, nosing for its way out. It had been penned up inside me too long, watching, waiting. My own strange and terrible companion.

You weren't so special, it whispered coldly to me. *You weren't one of a kind.*

After all, we were brothers, you and I. While you let your Dolittle roam wild and free—making you only *seem* stronger, better—after Mama died, I'd yoked mine to the fear and guilt of my terrible secret: A jumpy colt that heeded me in a childish fit of temper at not being allowed to ride him. Mama was dead because of me—*because of what I could do*—and ever since then I'd kept my own deadly Dolittle caged and seething, mostly docile, yet never fully tamed.

But no more. No more.

Corporal's barking transformed into a kind of terrible machine gun that fired in rhythm with my heartbeat—*thump, thump, thump*—as if the trigger inside me were being pulled tighter and tighter—*thump, thump, thump*—until at last, in that simple, perfect communion that I've come to dread and cherish in all the years since, his rage became my rage, and my rage, his.

Thump, thump, thump.

I reached up and yanked the brass question mark.

An ecstatic whoosh flooded into me.

Corporal and I leapt as one to freedom and were gone.

And then the silence. And then the scream.

I jerked upright, my bond with the dog broken, the bite of cold metal still burning my palm. The sound came again, no mistaking it now, your voice, shrill and penetrating, and so pitiful it nearly swamped me in a swell of horror.

I hurled myself to my feet and ran.

You kept howling my name, over and over, but at first, I couldn't see you. I couldn't see Corporal either. Couldn't see anything really, nor hear anything save the terrible sound of your shrieking louder, louder, louder.

I stumbled around the corner of the house and bolted across the driveway, nearly taking a header as I tripped over an old iron spade Hazzard had left lying in the grass. With a man-sized surge of adrenaline, I hauled its dead weight into my arms. But though I could barely keep from toppling over with that heavy thing clutched to my chest as I ran, I finally saw the orchard looming ahead, a sorry patch of misshapen trees that quivered in a spill of sickly light from the orange moon cresting Connecticut Hill.

There you were, kneeling on the ground, a struggling mass of boy and dog wrangling for dear life at the feet of those twisted trees. Swarms of crows and starlings dived and pecked wildly at Corporal's body, but it was no use: The Rottweiler had you by the forearm, his canines sunk fast into the meat of you. The basket lay useless by your side as you bellowed for my help, beating the animal over the head with your free fist. But he'd dug so deeply into your flesh I thought he'd rip your arm clean off before he let you go. His grudge was that unquenchable.

My grudge.

That's when I knew he'd never give you up—I *knew* it—and in the cruel clarity of that moment, as I reckoned with my childish impotence at how to stop what I'd unleashed, I also knew I'd have to kill him if I wanted to save you.

Thus, with all the strength I could muster, I heaved that rusty spade over my head and brought it down with a sickening thud against Corporal's writhing back.

The birds scattered.

The recoil was stunning. Pain jolted through my body. I lost my grip and the spade tumbled to the ground.

Corporal released your arm and staggered backwards, but before I could reach down to pull you to your feet, he'd shaken off my blow and launched himself back at you.

In an instant of absolute silence, he had you by the throat.

You collapsed back into the grass and went limp.

My lungs exploded in a wail.

I threw myself on top of him, dug my fingers into his eyes, but though he whimpered and whined, he would not release you.

I scrambled back to my feet and dove for the spade. I hoisted it above my head and brought the edge of the blade down sharply against the base of Corporal's skull. Vertebrae crackled like kindling. Jets of blood spurted from a gash in his fur. He twitched in a violent fit and then his body deflated against yours, his teeth still embedded in your neck.

I threw myself onto the two of you, driving my fingers into Corporal's slippery mouth until I'd pried apart his jaws and pushed him off you. You began to convulse then, the air rich with the tang of your blood. But at least you were still breathing, the shallow rise of your chest matched by a moist sucking that escaped the terrible gore in your throat.

I got behind you and jimmied my fingers into your armpits to try to lift you, but you were just too heavy. Next, I tried to stop the bleeding with my small hands, but it was no use, and so I grabbed you by the ankles instead and managed to drag you back toward the house, to a phone, an adult. Still, it never occurred to me to drop you and run for help. It never crossed my mind that that was maybe the only way to save your life. Christ, I was just a boy covered in my brother's blood. All I knew was that I couldn't leave you, not after what had happened.

Not after what I'd done.

So, I didn't leave you. Not as I watched your face drain of color in the rising moonlight. Not as the woods erupted in a mournful chorus of yowls and caws and screeches. Not as your skin turned cold, then waxy, and the blood stopped pumping from your throat. Not once during those minutes that turned to hours and then lifetimes did I move from your side. Not until I finally heard the approaching thrum of Hazzard's pickup.

"Hang on," I whispered futilely into your ear. "Hang on."

Only then did I abandoned your ashen corpse to run for the sound of that truck.

But before that moment, back before that night became superimposed on everything that's happened since. Before the rages, the therapy, the self-loathing. Before my nightmares of you and Mama and the others made sleep all but impossible. Before the blood—*oh, the blood*—and all these deaths, the terrible price for what I've become without you. Back before any of that, as we huddled together beneath the moonlight, you and I, back with the fingers of darkness poised to close around us forever. Somewhere in those final moments we spent together, I came to understand one excruciating truth:

    I was the only one now.

    And deep down, dear brother, I was glad of it.

The Njogel

I looked up from my book that night to find the Njogel peering down at me through my bedroom window, his black horse's nostrils exhaling whorls of blue fog into the frigid air. I kicked away my blankets, sat up on my heels, pressed my fingertips to the glass as if to reach through it to caress his muzzle. In the moon glow I caught sight of my own reflection. The snow light had turned my skin pale blue, and for a moment I thought I must be staring at my own ghost. But no, not yet, though I knew that's why he'd finally come for me, that reaper of the deep I'd longed for on so many terrible nights without you.

You see, baby, after you were gone, I researched him for months in all the books you left behind. I learned what I must do when he came for me. I tried all the recommended ways to call him. The dream chants. The whispers into the wind. The small creatures sacrificed on the riverbank. But for so many nights he disappointed me, until I'd almost lost hope that the old, tired magic would even work anymore.

But here he was, finally, and instead of feeling bitter that he'd made me wait for so long, the reflected me who gazed out with wonder at the water horse come to carry me to the bottom of the cold, dead river merely looked relieved to finally be going.

And what of the Njogel himself? His coat was the inky black of drowning in deep water. Though the night was calm, a phantom gale lashed his mane like seaweed caught in an angry riptide. The muscles of his neck and flanks rippled with raw power, yet his eyes were not fearsome at all, merely glazed and cloudy like that of a dead thing washed up on a desolate shore. He neighed a thunderous greeting to me, and the walls of the trailer quivered like a storm-lashed hull. Then he swept his broad horse's head in an invitation, and my aching for you carried me out of my bed and into the living room, where I was bathed in blue light from the television.

Mama laid sprawled like a crime scene in her recliner, her hand still glued to the rim of an empty China teacup that hadn't seen tea since before Daddy died. She'd tried to "talk sense" into me many times after you were gone. She grew concerned over my obsession.

She said, "Boy, let the dead bury their dead."

She said, "My God, don't end up like me."

But these were just empty words. We both knew we mourned our ghosts with our whole bodies and souls. It was in our blood, and I could no more stop burning on the inside for you than she might will herself sober.

Haunted was what we'd become.

It was then that I noticed that the left side of her robe had come undone, exposing a crumpled wad of brown-bag breast. I moved to cover her with an afghan, but the Njogel battered his muzzle impatiently against the trailer, pitching it into such a violent shimmy that I had to leave Mama to her indecency and hurry outside.

The night air struck me breathless. A rime of frost crusted the trailer's metal walls, which glinted like stardust in the moonlight. A breeze rattled the silvered bones of the trees, carrying with it the stench of the rotting river bottom. The Njogel strode toward me, his eyes fixed upon me, luring me toward him, turning my naked skin to gooseflesh. He neighed again, and the sound of it sent an electric pulse coursing through my body. He scratched at the frozen ground with a backward-turned hoof, and then bowed his head in fealty and knelt before me.

I approached him slowly, wincing as icy pebbles bit into the soles of my bare feet. Yet the Njogel remained still, perhaps fearing I would bolt at any sudden movement. But although he was huge and menacing, mightier than I could've imagined, I was not afraid. Why should I be? The only thing I had left to lose was the very thing I'd called him here to take from me.

When I finally bent forward to whisper my request into his ear, the whole world hushed as if leaning in to eavesdrop. "I am Samuel Amon Williams," I said, my voice as calm and fearless as all the books had instructed it to be. "I give you my one true name of my own free will. And now you must do for me what you've come here to do. Take me to him. Take me to the boy I love. Take me to the bottom of that cold, dead river, so that we may be together again."

But baby, when I twisted my fingers into the Njogel's icy mane to mount him, he just melted into nothing in my grasp.

His body vanished, gone.

All I was left holding onto in that barren moonlight was your soft, black peacoat.

*

I wear it sometimes now when I'm alone. It helps me to think of you as you once were. It reminds me of what we had back then, how beautiful you were, how tender with me, how strong. Of course, I can't let anyone see that I have it. How could I explain? I read the police report, the witness statements. How you were wearing it when those animals chased you onto the bridge, screaming "Faggot" and "Spook" and "Devil lover." How they cornered you, kicked you and beat you, sliced your poor naked throat and then hurled your battered body into the cold, black river.

But it doesn't even smell of your blood anymore.

Not of wet or rot or the stink of the river bottom.

Now it smells only of you.

Of your incense. Of your sweat. Of your dollar store shampoo.

It smells of your smile.

Sometimes I sleep with it draped over the top of me.

Sometimes, late at night, I carry it in my backpack down to the river bank. Once there, I lovingly unfold it from the bag. Then I strip naked, slip it over my bare shoulders, and stride boldly into that bitter black water.

The slime and silt at the bottom suck at my toes. The wind whips the waves into a frenzy. Moonlight cascades down from the inky sky, catching in the Njogel's mane like stardust as he emerges from the deeper water to greet me. Then he lets me clamber onto his mighty back, and with a thunderous bray that shatters the night, together we ride, ride, ride …

Jill

When I woke up yesterday morning, I saw how Mom had spelled out HELL IS OTHER PEOPLE in magnetic poetry on the fridge before she left for work. It was a stupid thing to write. I knew from hunting with Jill what real hell looked like.

But I also knew what Mom really meant: HELL IS LIVING WITH MY WORTHLESS LARD ASS SON WHO STAYS OUT ALL NIGHT, EATS ME OUT OF HOUSE AND HOME, AND NEVER MINDS A SINGLE WORD I SAY. She just didn't have the words and letters to spell all that.

There are never enough words and letters to fill the gaps between us.

Still, it got her point across just fine, and since I wasn't in any hurry to get to first period study hall, I took my sweet time rearranging the pieces to say LOVE MEANS NEVER HAVING TO SAY YOUR SORRY. I knew it would piss off her because it's something Jill likes to say. I'm not even sure what it's supposed to mean.

Jill just says it.

9

It was Jill who got her mother to give me my job down at Pancake Chalet.

It was during those six months when she and Mom were best A.A. buddies or whatever, and Mom kept bugging her to find me something to do to get me off my fat ass and out of her refrigerator. I'm not the kind to do whatever Mom tells me to do, though. The only reason I showed up to interview with Mrs. Hachette was because I wanted the job for myself. To earn some cash to get my own wheels before graduation, and so I wouldn't have to beg for a ten spot every time I felt like going to a movie.

I could tell right away Mrs. Hachette didn't like me. But I didn't care because she still gave me the job. So what if it was only because Jill made her? She does whatever Jill wants, on account of Jill being adopted and troubled, with an "addictive personality disorder," or whatever that expensive shrink she goes to tells her.

Mrs. Hachette will do anything to keep Jill on the wagon.

I say, if she made sure the wagon was a bloodmobile, she'd have a shot at that.

Anyway, it doesn't matter that the old lady doesn't like me. Jill warned her to back off, and she did. She doesn't glare over my shoulder while I run the dish machine anymore. She's stopped clocking my breaks. She lets me work weeknights and closings now, instead of just Saturday and Sunday rush. She pays me under the table and didn't even make me go through the hassle of getting a work permit. So what if she treats me like a maggot she found squirming in a pile of dog shit? It's $250 a week in my pocket, and it gets me out from under Mom's thumb, so I'm fine with her dirty looks and fine with Mrs. Hachette.

Of course, she doesn't know a thing about me and Jill. It would be hell to pay if she found out. She doesn't know how, after closing sometimes, when the cooks and waitstaff have all gone home, Jill and I eat the best steaks straight out of the cooler, raw. Then we get smashed on B.V. and Coke and make out in the squeaky vinyl booths where hours before little kids dribbled their canned cherry compote, their slender throats pulsing, pulsing. Mrs. Hachette doesn't know how we undress each other in the stock room so we can open little red slits in our skin with that sweet, spring-loaded knife-ring Jill got off of eBay. Then we drink from each other's bodies to seal our bond. I like to sip from Jill's breasts and her soft belly. She likes hers to come fresh from my love handles or the fleshy insides of my thighs.

Afterwards, we do whippets in the cooler until the walls vibrate and my eyes feel like they're going to pop like firecrackers. Mrs. Hachette must wonder why Pancake Chalet goes through so many cases of Ready Whip.

But then again, I bet she probably doesn't want to know.

8

Janice is in the backseat bitching about the price of the cigarettes she just bought at the Nice 'N Easy. To shut her up, Jill makes a big show out of sliding her hand up the inside of my thigh to squeeze my junk, which is like, duh, perfectly okay by me.

Actually, everything Jill does is okay by me.

But Janice ignores her and begins howling instead that she wants her kick, and by that she means a toot, and by that, I mean a snort, and, well, everybody knows what that means, right? But Jill is all like, "Later," which means when she's good and ready and not a minute sooner, and I'm perfectly okay with that because I'm not in the mood for them to get all coked up tonight.

Not now. Not ever.

The streetlights flash past the windshield like lightning bolts, while the engine rumbles like a thundercloud. I'm feeling electric. No work tonight, no school in the morning, and after midnight we hunt. Plus, I love riding shotgun with Jill. Her car is this sweet piece of Detroit's finest: a shiny, Guido-black Chrysler 300, with 20-inch aluminum wheels, power everything, a black leather interior that smells like hot summer sex, and an enormous trunk that even I can fit inside. Jill lets me drive it sometimes, late at night when there's no traffic around or she's too fucked-up to care. Mrs. Hachette bought it for her as a reward for graduating from that fancy rehab downstate. It's got all-wheel drive and the Hemi V8, so the thing can haul ass. Though it's no Corvette, it's still way better than Mom's POS Elantra.

The best part is that Jill won't let Janice drive it anymore, on account of it was Janice who totaled her old Caddy that night on their way home from scoring beans at some gay club in Syracuse when the Thruway was a sheet of ice.

I love how Janice's face squeezes up like a fist whenever Jill tosses me the keys.

The night air rushes in like a river through the open window. Jill is easily doing eighty-five down the Arterial. She loves going fast and knows the 300 can handle it. She weaves around the other cars like they're not even moving, like they're elephants, and we're riding the back of a black and chrome cheetah. She won't get a ticket either. Not in this county. The cops don't even bother pulling her over anymore for all the grief it causes. One call to her brother and it's done: Sorry for the trouble Ms. Hachette ... Have a good evening, Ms. Hachette ... Give my best to your brother, Ms. Hachette.

Jill knows she owns this town. I guess we all do.

But that doesn't even matter now. All that matters is how electric I feel. Like, I have this sense that something's going to happen tonight, something wild and unexpected. I always feel this way before a hunt, like life is a fiery jolt of possibility, and everything is real and alive and good. I mean, we're good, me and Jill. Jill and me. I think this is what happiness is supposed to feel like. This real, alive feeling, our blood pulsing hot through each other's veins. Knowing that what's there between us is an actual, honest-to-God thing. Not some daydream. Not some high school jerk-off fantasy. But the real deal, here and now.

Me and Jill. Jill and me.

7

I told Mom at breakfast last Saturday that this girl I know from work said she thought I was handsome. Mom just snorted, said "Whatever," and took another drag off her Pall Mall. I didn't tell her that it was Jill, but it irritated her, nonetheless. She leaned over the table and pinched my nipple hard and said she didn't care what some blind tramp told me, she expected me to wear a shirt when I sat at her kitchen table, because she didn't want to stare at my hairy moobs while she ate her fried eggs.

She didn't even ask about all the scars.

Anyway, I ignored her. I figured I was entitled to enjoy my secrets, and so I leaned back in my chair and scratched my bare chest like I didn't have a care in the world.

Since Jill and me started hooking up, I don't wear shirts as much as I used to. Even mowing the grass outside where everyone can see. It's not because I suddenly think I'm good looking. I know I'm just as fat and pasty as ever. My hair is still gnarly, I still have shitty posture, and my, um, junk could be bigger. I mean, I guess every dude thinks that, right? But I'm pretty sure I'm not batting with the major leaguers down there. I've looked in the locker room before, which is totally normal and doesn't mean anything gay. It's like when you're driving a hot car and some dude pulls up next to you in another hot car and you check each other out. It's natural, like in the jungle, survival of the fittest, Darwin and shit.

Still, I guess it's okay that I'm not King Dong, because Jill she says she likes it that way. It makes me her eager little beaver. She says hung dudes think they don't have to try. They make the woman do all the work. But not me. I do whatever she tells me to do for as long as she tells me to do it. Fingers. Lips. Tongue. She says I don't need a big dick to make her feel good, and then she whispers in my ear that it's all good, that everything I do feels good to her.

And then we open our veins and drink from each other, and it's good.

I mean, all good.

Everything is good with Jill.

6

Janice is being such a whiny bitch tonight.

I feel her eyes burning holes into on the back of my head while she complains about me riding shotgun. It's always something with her: too hot or too cold, they raised the price of Merit's, she's PMSing hard, or she's just sick of looking at my face. It's like she thinks we're holding out on her, like Jill's got a secret stash of coke in the glove compartment or she's shoved a bag of it up my ass.

But Janice can go fuck herself.

She's pushing fifty for Christ's sake. Practically old enough to be my grandmother, yet she acts like a spoiled brat whenever I'm around. I guess it's because she thinks I'm standing between her and Jill. Maybe I am, though I'm pretty sure Jill was done with her dyke phase after she and Mom broke things off.

I don't even understand why Jill still hangs out with Janice. She blows her off at work, keeping to the hostess station whenever Janice is behind the grill. They never talk, except when Jill starts jonesing to hunt or needs somebody to go with her to her shrink appointments. Back when they were A.A. buddies, Mom said she thought Jill kept losers like Janice around because they made her feel better about herself. I wanted to ask, if that was true, why she thought Jill kept her around? But I wasn't suicidal. Besides, she was right. I figure it's not such a bad thing if you're Jill to hang around a loser like Janice, who does whatever you say and acts as if the sun rises and sets when you tell it to.

Still, I feel bad for Janice sometimes. It's obvious she's nursing a major ache for Jill. Sometimes it hurts to look at her, like when Jill kisses me or touches me, and I can see through all that rage to the sadness buried in Janice's eyes.

Other times, though, like when she's being a bitch to me, I'm happy to see her suffer.

Like, this one night, she got all wasted on blood and coke and vodka after the hunt, and she started joking around about how stupid Dad was to get busted holding onto the murder weapon after he fled the bar that night. I don't let anybody talk shit about Dad—except Mom—so I grabbed her by the throat and nearly choked her out.

She never mentioned him again after that.

So, whatever. Let her bitch and moan. She can just sit there and wait for her damn buzz until after the hunt.

It's not even 11:00 yet, and I'm so not ready to watch the two of them get all coked up even before we grab the kid. When the two of them get high it turns into this scene out of Scarface, except without Pacino and the guns. Janice starts pacing around her trailer like a rat in a cage, all hyper and crazy, while Jill just stares through the window blinds like she thinks she's being staked-out or something. If a phone rings, forget about it: It's like the FBI is about to break down the door.

It's so stupid and pointless.

I mean, Jill doesn't have a thing to worry about from the law. Her brother's the goddamned D.A. and will probably be the next mayor: She could slash a guy's throat on the courthouse steps, and the cops would just go shoot some poor Black dude for jaywalking.

5

On my seventeenth birthday, I woke up to find that Mom had spelled out YOUR FIRST WORD WAS COOKIE on the fridge as my happy birthday poem. Beside it she'd duct-taped a small mirror to the door handle.

Looking in that mirror was the first time I realized my tits were bigger than hers.

I Googled it that afternoon. Gy·ne·co·mas·ti·a: *American Heritage* defined it as "Abnormal enlargement of the breasts in a male."

Mom just calls it being a lard ass.

When I told Jill about it later that night, she said that when Mrs. Hachette dies and she comes into her big inheritance, she'll give me the cash I need for plastic surgery to chop off my moobs, so long as we can find a doctor who'll let us keep the meat afterwards.

Then she laughed.

Jill says my body doesn't matter to her. She says she likes how warm and juicy I am, how she can bleed me for hours without me passing out. She says it all feels the same in the dark anyway, and besides, being fat doesn't make me less of a man.

She says a lot of things like that. Things I don't believe, but I pretend like I do. I guess it's sweet of her to say them, to try to spare my feelings. It's just her way of showing she cares, so the least I could do is act like I believe her.

Besides, Jill likes to say that it's perfectly okay with God and the universe when you lie, so long as you do it out of love or self-preservation. Who can fault her when you look at it like that? Self-preservation is just part of the natural law, like survival of the fittest or whatever. And as for the love part, doesn't that mean you're never supposed to say you're sorry, even for lying or worse? Especially for worse.

Later on that same night, after she gave me my special birthday blow job, I asked her if she thought we were maybe in love, and she sat up in the driver's seat with this dead look in her eyes and said, "Why don't you tell me?"

Christ! What the hell was I supposed to say to that? It wasn't like there was some easy, obvious answer to give her. Sure, I kind of thought maybe I did love her, at least a little. I certainly liked her a lot, and besides, it wasn't as if I'd gone around drinking blood and hunting with all these other women. We were spending all this time together, and it was good, and I was having fun. It was nice and different and unexpected to have somebody cool who wanted to be around me as much as I wanted to be around them, which was such a change from the way things usually worked for me. Plus, what a sweet little bonus that she had a nice car, tons of cash, and was old enough to buy liquor.

But even more than that, it seemed like we'd connected in this deep, mysterious way, you know? Or at least, I thought we had. I'd told her everything about Dad, and she told me all about what it was like being the screw-up in the otherwise sitcom-perfect, all-American family. She even hinted at some of the sick shit Mom said had gone down between her and her old man before he died. The stuff nobody was supposed to know about except Jill's shrink and Mrs. Hachette, who apparently had to keep bribing her daughter with cars and money and rehab just so she could live with herself for letting it happen in the first place.

So yeah, maybe I did kind of love Jill, even if she lied to my face about paying for my moob surgery, or about not caring that I was a lard ass, or that she and Mom had only been A.A. buddies before their big blowup. But I wasn't about to tell her any of that. Hell no. Or at least, I wasn't going to be the first to commit to that fucking loser's word out loud.

Love? I'm not that stupid.

So, instead of answering her, I just did what I always do when I don't know what else to say to her: I shrugged and offered up a vein in my arm.

4

The first time is the one I remember best.

It began on this random Thursday night, after we were done closing a few weeks into my evening shifts at Pancake Chalet. Jill called me into the office after everyone had left. She wore this shit-eating grin on her face and told me I looked tired and burned out. Wouldn't I like a little kick? A little pick-me-up to get the rest of the night going?

I just figured she had some blow to offer, and so I was like, "Sure, whatever."

She laughed in her lifeless way, and then made me swear not to narc, that this was our little secret, blah, blah, blah. But once I'd sworn, instead of pulling out a bullet of coke from her purse, she flicked the hidden button on her ring, dragged the little blade across the back of her arm, and offered it up for me to drink.

For a minute I just stood there and gawped at her. I guess I was freaked out or something. But she held me in that cool, steady gaze of hers, and then it wasn't so bad anymore, and I stopped being afraid.

Instead, I leaned forward and drank.

To be honest, it was gross at first. The blood tasted all hot and metallic, and right away I wanted to gag. But she held the back of my head in place with her other hand and kept moaning for me to drink more, more, more, until all at once, the whole experience shifted. I got this crazy-intense rush of energy, and suddenly I was ready to kick ass and take names or some redneck shit like that. My body felt tingly and alive in this hyper-aware sort of way, like everything was super sharp and crystal clear and under my control.

That was the main thing, really: control. All of a sudden it felt like the kind of dude who actually had some say over his own life. It's amazing what a few sips of fresh blood can trick your brain into believing. It was like waking up to the sunrise after a whole lifetime spent locked in a casket. I no longer felt like the fat, lonely loser from The Flats who'd gotten his ass kicked practically every day since he was ten, because everybody knew his Mom was a drunk and his old man got sent down to Elmira for first-degree manslaughter.

Instead, the me I saw was some badass dude I barely recognized. I was drinking the blood of rich, older women now. I had secrets, real ones. Not kid's stuff. Not high-school-drama-club bullshit. No, these were bona fide, grown-up secrets—the kind they made sexy vampire flicks about—and it was as if Jill had taken me behind a velvet rope, where the only price of admission was letting her slurp a pint of her own from me.

Anyway, after we'd finished drinking, we locked up the restaurant and went for a drive. We weren't even looking to hook up right away. We were still feeling each other out, getting to know one another, and anyway sometimes the blood just really makes you want to drive and talk.

So, we drove and talked.

I don't remember now much of what we said. But what I do remember was realizing how, despite her being Mom's age and all, Jill was actually hot. Or, not hot exactly, but beautiful, you know? In the headlights of the passing cars, her green eyes glinted like broken glass. Her hair was soft and feathery, shimmering like a field of wheat in the wind. I wanted to reach over and touch it, though I didn't dare, so I just stared at it—at her, I mean—and talked and talked, and gazed into her face because it seemed to glow in the passing headlights, with the stars above us in the sky, and maybe the moon, too, and the soft yellow shimmer of the streetlights, and the city all around us, holding its breath to listen as we laughed and talked and talked.

It was nice. Really nice.

Or, maybe... I dunno.

It was probably just the blood.

Anyway, whatever it was, it felt really good while it lasted. But then she said it was time for us to go hunting with Janice, and the night turned like bad weather.

By the time we got to Janice's trailer way out in the boonies, we were late, and Janice had already put to bed a six pack of Utica Club. As soon as she opened the door, she let me know how unhappy she was to see me. But what could she do about it? Jill wanted me there. It was Jill's car, Jill's plan, Jill's hunt. Janice and I were just along for the ride.

So anyway, we all climbed into the 300 and went to pick up the kid. It was all so new to me at that point, I mostly kept my mouth shut and did what I was told. Jill had already made plans to meet him at this vacant lot near the train tracks. It's a different location each time. She knows the city like the back of her hand, so it's a simple enough thing for her to tell them to meet us where there's no cops or security cameras around. And okay, so I guess that means it's technically not a "hunt," since it's always prearranged like this.

Maybe it's more like a takeout run to pick up a late-night order?

Anyway, Jill usually finds the kids on Tenchat, or one of the other encrypted apps that are impossible to trace. She has a real nose for sniffing out the needy ones. She chats them up, gets to know them, gets them to reveal their secrets and desires, frustrations, routines. Sometimes it takes her weeks to groom them before she finally lowers the boom.

They're always the same, too: lonely, bored, broke, and horny.

The boys are easier. All she has to do is flash a tit and some coke and they hop right into the car as soon as we show up. The girls sometimes change their minds when they see me and Janice. If they try to put up a fight, I'm there to make sure they cooperate, or else they end up in the trunk.

The rest is straightforward. When we get back to Janice's trailer, Jill takes them into the bedroom, fucks around with them awhile, and then pump's them so full of shit their hearts stop beating in minutes.

Next, the three of us get to work.

Janice has the tools already laid out in the bathroom, so we just have to dump the body into the tub, get undressed, and then we drink and drink and eat and fuck.

After that, it usually takes a couple of hours to chop up what's left and clean up the mess. Jill gets rid of their phones on her way home. I don't know what Janice does with the clothes, but Jill gave her some cash to buy this huge chest freezer to store the extra meat, so there's always leftovers to defrost whenever we get a craving. There are at least two or three of them stuffed in that freezer right now. If you ask me, that's why Jill prefers kids. They're smaller, so we can fit more inside. Plus, she claims the flesh is tender.

Janice says Jill just likes them young.

Anyway, this kid said his name was Kyle. He claimed to be seventeen, but I could tell he was more like thirteen or fourteen. Although he was short, he was built like a wrestler with washboard abs or whatever, plus this wavy black hair and the piecing blue eyes of a boy-band singer. I saw later on that he had a big dick, too, so I was glad when we ate him.

But then Jill had to break out the coke and that ruined everything.

I just wanted to spend some quality time alone with her, you know? Cuddling or whatever. But she and Janice had to go get all fucked up without me. Janice turned on the TV, and they started to pace around the living room, rehashing the kill while a *Family Guy* rerun blared in the background. Jill offered me some blow, but I didn't want any, even though I'd started to feel weirdly depressed. More so than usual. Maybe it was all that blood or coming down off the high of the hunt. Or maybe it was just because I'd experienced this totally amazing connection with Jill earlier in the night that'd suddenly switched off for no good reason.

Actually, it was more like she'd switched off. Right there in front of me. One minute she was totally into me, and the next she'd slipped back inside herself. It was like I wasn't even in the room anymore. I guess that hurt me or whatever, because then the usual dark shit swirling inside my head turned really dark. Like, scary dark. I started crawling out of my skin and imagining doing something bad to myself. My heart couldn't stop racing, and my brain wouldn't stop running through all these random, ugly thoughts, like remembering that time I was asleep and Mom woke me up in nothing but her panties, slobbering drunk and sobbing that she'd ruined our lives by shacking up with a killer like Dad. Or the time Mike Sweeney stole my clothes in gym class and stuffed them into the toilet with his turd, and I had to wear my smelly gym clothes the rest of the day because Mom couldn't get out of work. Or the time my bike got stolen from the backyard, but Mom wouldn't call the cops, even though we knew who'd swiped it, because she was wasted and terrified the pigs would take me away from her, too.

So, there I was, wigging out over all these pointless, fucked-up memories, only I couldn't do anything to stop it. I started to sweat, right through my clothes. I couldn't stop cracking my knuckles or sit still, and I hadn't even snorted any coke.

I think I maybe even started to cry.

By then, they'd finished off the last bullet, so Jill passed me a bottle of vodka to even me out. But it only made me sick to my stomach, what with all that blood and Kyle-meat down there, and so I had to go puke in the kitchen sink, because Janice had freaked out over something Jill said about me spending the night and had locked herself in the bathroom.

After that, all I wanted to do was go home and sleep it off. But Jill wouldn't leave, so I ended up walking the whole six miles in the dark, and when I finally got home before dawn, I couldn't even fall asleep, which totally sucked because I had to get up for school in a few hours to take this test on *Of Mice and Men* that for once I didn't want to blow off because I'd actually read the damn book.

3

This morning's poem said DO NOT TAKE WHAT DOES NOT BELONG TO YOU.

At first, I didn't know what the hell Mom was talking about, because I make it a point never to touch her shit. It's nothing but grief when I do.

But then I remembered how Jill had lifted a pack of her cigarettes from the carton in the fridge when she picked me up for work yesterday.

She had a smirk as wide as a dinner plate on her face when she did it.

Jill gets off on taking what doesn't belong to her. Like, she's always laughing about how she lifts all this crap from the storeroom at Pancake Chalet. Crazy, useless shit. Cases of non-dairy creamers, industrial cans of Hollandaise sauce, plastic bags filled with steel wool pads. Stuff she knows she'll never use in a million years. I think she hurls it all into the dumpster behind her apartment building as soon as she gets home at night. It's kind of stupid and wasteful, but it's totally hysterical, too. Like, what ridiculous thing will she steal next, you know? I guess it's not really stealing though, since Mrs. Hachette owns the place, so all that stuff really sort of belongs to Jill in a way.

It's all in the family or whatever.

Anyway, it really pissed me off that Mom thought I stole her cigarettes, but I didn't want her to know that it was actually Jill. She'd kill me if she found out I let Jill back into our place. So instead, I spelled out MY HEART BELONGS TO DADDY, because it was a line in a song from some old movie I saw on TV, and because she hates it whenever I bring him up. Almost as much as she hates it when I mention Jill.

The thing is, I still don't know what went down between the two of them.

I know there's more of a story there, but I don't want to hear it.

I don't like to think of Mom and Jill drinking each other's blood.

I want that to be just for Jill and me.

It's not like I could ask Mom anyway, and when I'm alone with Jill, the last thing on my mind is home, even though once in a while she'll bring Mom up. Her face will go all tight, and she'll ask me stupid shit, like how's Mom doing at work or if she's seeing anybody new. It's almost like she's jealous or maybe missing her a little. It makes me super uncomfortable, and though I only toss her off one-word answers, she never presses me for details and lets it drop, which is fine by me.

The way I figure it, her secrets with Mom are none of my business. They don't belong to me, any more than Mom's cigarettes do, and I don't take what doesn't belong to me, no matter what Mom thinks.

Jill has lots of other secrets, too. But they're all ones I don't ask about and don't need to know. She tells me what she feels like telling me. I don't pry after the rest. I think it's why we have this deep connection. It's like respect, you know? Her secrets are cool with me. I've lived practically my whole life without any of my own, so I know how lucky she is to still have hers. Since Dad got sent down, my entire life has felt like this trashy novel that everybody in town has read, laughed at, and tossed into the garbage. I think the world would be a better place if more people just minded their own fucking business. I really don't need to know Jill's private business, like what she talks about with her shrink, or the gory details about her and her father, or why she won't ever let me touch her or kiss her or even hold her hand until after we've opened each other's veins and taken our first slurp.

I mean, it doesn't really bother me. Not really. Not too much.

Anyway, it's cool and all, because the way I see it, secrets are like lies: When you keep them, it's almost always out of love or self-preservation.

2

It's not like Jill hasn't done eighty-five down this stretch of the Arterial a thousand times before, so I have no idea why we got pulled over tonight, except that the cop's a rookie and maybe didn't recognize her car or know who the brother of the woman driving it was.

When she saw the flashing red lights in her rearview mirror, Jill cursed about us being late to pick up this girl named Wendy she'd arranged to meet for tonight's fun. Then she refused to pull over until I'd deleted all the chat apps from her phone.

"Just in case," she said.

As soon as she'd stopped the car, she jumped out and started giving the rookie a hard time. If she'd been a Black dude, he probably would have shot her on the spot. But he clearly didn't know what do about a belligerent, thirty-something White lady yelling her brother's name over and over and saying, "Don't you know who I am?"

Finally, he called for backup.

While all this was happening, Janice sat behind me rocking back and forth, muttering, "Don't narc, don't narc, don't narc," under her breath. I could see in the rearview mirror that her face had gone as white as death.

As white as Mom's did on the day they sentenced Dad.

That was the only time I ever saw Jill's brother in person. He was just Assistant D.A. then, and I remember how he nodded at me and Mom as he left the courtroom, like it was nothing personal, you know? Like it was just business or whatever. Though that was years before Jill and Mom and me, it was a good thing he never came around to Pancake Chalet, because even though I knew he wouldn't recognize me, I still didn't want him to see me.

But as we sat there waiting for the backup cop to show, I started to freak out thinking that this time he might actually have to come down to bail out his little sister from her scrape with the law, and then he would see me, and remember who I was, and lock me up just for the hell of it, because Mom says that's what they do to trash like us.

When the backup cop finally showed, I could tell right away that Jill was happy to see him. She smiled this big, shit-eating grin and waved to him the minute he stepped out of his cruiser. He was a lot older than the rookie, and after a private chit-chat with the kid, he strode over to Jill like Mr. Big Swinging Dick and threw his arm around her all fatherly. Then they started chatting and laughing, and I was so relieved that this shit was finally over.

But then his phone rang, and after a moment of speaking to whoever it was on the line, he handed it to Jill, and that's when everything turned dark.

I can't really say that I've never seen Jill look more scared than she did taking that phone from him, because, well, I'd never actually seen Jill scared at all. Sure, she'd been crazy, twitchy paranoid from being strung-out before. But never stone-sober, white-as-death petrified. This was the first time, and seeing her expression change so swiftly like that made me feel as if the bottom had dropped out of the world.

She didn't say much to whoever was on the other end of the call, just nodded a few times and whispered, and then handed the phone back to the cop. Maybe it was her brother. Maybe he'd gotten sick of bailing her ass out. Truth is, I don't know who it was, but as soon as the cop hung up, he grabbed Jill by the elbow, and still all fatherly-like, walked her to the far side of his cruiser, where they whispered to each other for a long while.

He reached into his pocket for his cigarettes and lit one for her.

I could tell she was trying really hard not to look at me or Janice.

Janice was still rocking back and forth behind me whispering, "Don't narc, don't narc, don't narc," but I knew it was already too late for that.

Then Jill said something to the cop, who gestured to the rookie, who came over to the passenger side with his hand on his weapon and ordered us to get out of the car slowly, with our hands up.

1

But I can barely move because I'm shaking so hard.

My hands are quaking, my knees, too, and the rookie notices this and gives me a big, fat grin, like he just won fifty bucks on a scratch-off.

Still, I manage to scramble out of the car without falling on my ass or getting shot.

Janice follows me out.

He makes us both lean face-down and arms spread against the hood, and frisks us slowly and carefully, asking before he turns out our pockets whether we've got anything sharp inside.

All he finds on me are my phone and wallet, which he sets on the hood beside me. I don't see what he pulls from Janice's pockets, because he sets it on the far side of her.

By now, the older cop has come over to watch the show. He mumbles something to the rookie about an eyewitness, a license plate, and a missing persons report. Then he picks up my wallet and flips it open, though I can tell he doesn't even look inside.

"So, you're Phil Rizzo's kid, huh?" he says, and I wonder how in the hell he knows that, until I glance over at Jill. She's still leaning against the cop car, smoking her cigarette and staring really hard at some distant fixed point down the road, like she's waiting on a cab to come take her to her shrink or the liquor store.

I want to call out to her, but I know it's too late for that. I could burst into flames right here and now, and she wouldn't even turn her head to look.

"Apple doesn't fall far from the tree, does it Mitch?" the older cop says to the rookie, who just shakes his head all smug, like, No, it sure doesn't. But when he's done frisking us, he turns to the older cop and tells him we're both clean, and for a moment I allow myself to think that we might be okay, that this might be the end of it after all, and shit, won't we have one hell of a story to laugh about later on, while we're snacking on Wendy's ribcage.

But no, because the older cop shakes his head, swaggers over to Jill, and whispers something else into her ear.

She doesn't say anything at first, just nods at him quickly, ever so slightly, and then mouths something I can't make out from so far away. Whatever it is though, it's all he needs, because he grins like the devil himself and flashes her a wink. A fucking wink! Like they're old buddies. Like they're sharing some secret, dirty joke at our expense.

Then he struts back over to me with his hand on his weapon and says, "The lady tells me you two've been borrowing her car late at night without her," and I swear to God, like, the first thought that pops into my head, the very first one, is that thing Jill always says, you know, about how love means never having to say you're sorry.

Well, I'm not sorry … I'm not sorry.

A Few Words from the New Tenant of ____ House

To Whom it May Concern:

I'm writing to inform you that I have recently moved into ____ House. I apologize for being circumspect about the name. I should probably just spit it out to make all of this easier, but what with copyright laws being as they are, it feels safer if I leave that to you to assume. I don't want to be sued for infringement! Besides, I'm fairly certain you are familiar enough with this particular house to discern its identity pretty easily on your own. It's rather famous, after all. If you haven't read the book, you've surely seen one of the films or the recent television series. Hint: it's that forsaken house on a hill made iconic by the phantom hand in the night, the bloody writing on the walls, the thing that walks alone there.

Except now, that thing has me for company.

Not that I ever dreamed I'd make ____ House my home. All I wanted when I opened the book was a change of scenery, you understand? A few hours refuge from the purgatory of this interminable quarantine and Mother's vicious sniping, especially if I could spend that time at a place with the spine-chilling reputation ____ House has. You see, I've always had an appetite for the macabre. Even when I was small, I was the sort of boy who pulled wings off of butterflies and incinerated ants on the sidewalk with a magnifying glass. I've spent my whole life rooting for the ghosts, ghouls, and monsters in my favorite novels.

For example, when I was eleven, I stole a paperback copy of *The Shining* from our local Goodwill and spent an entire weekend in delicious terror wishing I had my very own roque mallet, so that I could join Jack Torrance rampaging through the halls of the Overlook Hotel.

At thirteen, I sold my soul to the boy next door in exchange for an actual kiss, open-mouthed and with tongue, though when I pressed my luck and copped a feel between his legs, he slugged me in the gut so hard I saw stars. Then he tore to shreds the little slip of paper I'd given him with my name written out in my own blood.

That's what really broke my heart.

On my seventeenth birthday, I got arrested for reciting Poe by candlelight in the middle of the Salem Hill Cemetery. I'd dressed all in black, of course, and painted my fingernails especially for the occasion in a shade of blood-red called "Tell-Tale Heart." The cops didn't know what to make of me. They asked if I was there to smoke weed or kick over headstones, sacrifice kittens or to blow some old creeper I'd hooked up with on Grindr. How could I explain to them that I simply felt more at ease reading to the dead than skulking in the shadows of the Homecoming dance like some impotent Carrie White?

The dead do not laugh at me.

They listen.

Go ahead: call me a freak if you like. Everyone else

does, including Mother, but I enjoy that word very much. Freak: *One who is markedly unusual or abnormal.* That's from the *Webster's* definition, although when Mother screeches "FREAK!" at the top of her lungs as she clutches her rosary, I get a flame-in-the-belly satisfaction knowing I'm the one in our little nuclear meltdown of a family who's considered "markedly unusual and abnormal."

When she claims to pray for my soul's salvation, I don't even believe her.

Dear old Mother, with her pink fleece slippers and acid wash jeans. Her "Hang In There" calendars marked up with monthly novenas. Her jugs of Ernest & Julio Zinfandel stowed beneath the elastic-waist skirts in her closet where Jesus can't see, and the endless chain of her Merit Menthols, which, when I was smaller, somehow managed to find themselves occasionally snuffed out on my arms and back.

Ah, memories.

Every now and then I wonder if she misses me now that I'm living here full-time at _____ House. I doubt it. We're so little alike, after all. Me, with my books and dark thoughts, and her, with her parish suppers and 24/7 Fox News. Two atonal chords striking against each other in shrill cacophony, especially since the lockdowns began. Her life must seem so much more harmonious now without me trapped in it with her. Choirs of imaginary angels no doubt sing her to sleep each night.

I'd much prefer silence.

I have no friends who'll miss me here at _____ House, and while the WiFi is non-existent, it's not as if I pine for human connection anyway. I am not that kind of person. The enforced isolation of these past few months was never really a problem for me. Books are all the company I've ever desired. Besides, the Internet is just a mosh pit of nobodies brawling with each other to get noticed by a world that genuinely doesn't give a shit whether they live or die. That they all seem to know this and yet still endlessly bleat their thoughts and outrage into the void of cyberspace strikes me as rather pathetic. What's even worse is that with all of their selfies and tweets and posts, they've managed to squeeze nearly every drop of mystery out of living. Nothing is left sacred now, nothing private or unknown. There are no secret places on earth left to hide, nowhere one can become truly lost, though ever since I can remember that's all I've really wanted out of life: to lose myself.

To hide.

So that's why I came here, to ____ House, where the doors still refuse to remain sensibly shut. Sure, the place isn't particularly homey. It's stood empty for so long now the plumbing is perhaps the biggest nightmare of all. There are layers of dust on the furniture so thick they've congealed. No matter how many logs I burn in the fireplaces, the rooms remain inhumanly cold, so much so I can usually see my breath. The halls are as dark and gloomy as you'd imagine, only enlivened by the occasional bloody scrawl. Even the floors, though solid enough, creak and groan beneath the weightless footsteps of figures seen only as a flash in the mirror or a flutter in the corner of an eye. Phantom fists pound on my bedroom door at all hours, while disembodied cries rouse the hairs on my neck. Plus, I am awoken each midnight to the strains of the loneliest music in the world.

That's how I found myself dancing in the icy embrace of my new daemon lover.

We're a little family of two here at ___ House, he and I. *Journey's end in lovers meeting.*

"Your mother is glad you have disappeared, you know?"

This is what my daemon lover whispers into my ear while he ravishes me in the impenetrable gloom of a ____ House night. "She has always wished for you to be gone. Even before you were born, she was ashamed. Ashamed of her weakness. Ashamed she did not know the name of your father. Ashamed to be burdened with his bastard child. Though she prayed night and day for a miscarriage, she was too afraid of her church to end you herself. But now that you have disappeared, she is glad of your absence and longs for you never to return."

He's a bit of a stick in the mud, my daemon lover, what with his Victorian diction and reticence to share his softer side. But what does one expect from a tortured soul more than a century dead?

"Do you know how greatly she despises you?" he demands, and then howls his answer into the echo chamber of my skull with my very own voice: "Not nearly as much as I do!"

He says these hateful things to me as if I didn't already know them myself. But that's just his way. He led a hard life when he was still alive, what with his dead wives, sickly children, and questionable taste in home decor. I've made my allowances for the way he treats me now. If he's a tad cruel and takes pleasure in inflicting pain, it's only because life was cruel and painful to him back then. I understand this. I've lived through it myself. And though his words, like his caress, can be as bone-chilling as the grave, when we dance, I nevertheless feel his hunger for me pressed hard against my body, as burning hot as the Devil's own prick.

What more could I ask from a daemon lover?

Besides, unlike the living, he doesn't seem to mind that I'm overweight and unattractive, nor that I have a blaze of acne like a rain of brimstone down my back. It doesn't concern him that I hold a special communion with the darkness, nor does it embarrass him that I'd rather curl up with Lovecraft or Le Fanu than play football or drink beer and piss into a bonfire with my "buds." He's nonjudgmental about my sexuality, obviously, but also regarding my wardrobe choices and fondness for nail polish, and he would never, ever threaten to kick me out or disown me. I'm all he has here, and he means to keep me with him forever and ever. After all, what good is a daemon lover without a mortal's soul to possess and torment for eternity?

Thus, our arrangement suits me fine: I'd rather be desired than not any day.

So, I've settled in rather nicely, though it can be rather frightful here from time to time. But trust me, I'm not aiming for sympathy. It's merely the way things are these days. The world itself has become a frightful place. Death stalks the land. Evil reigns on high. Rage walks the streets. Holding onto some sort of stability, no matter how brutal or unwholesome it may be, seems far better to me than grasping at the sad tatters of nothing. If Mother's example has taught me anything, it's taught me that.

God is a dry tap.

No glorious new dawn awaits us at the turn of the calendar.

Jesus can't make me cum like Vesuvius, night after night after night.

Sometimes though, I wonder if Mother still thinks of me. Does she speculate where I've gone, if I'm succumbed to the virus, whether I'm safe or even happy? Has she noticed yet that I'm not even there? I occasionally imagine her pounding on my bedroom door, calling out my name repeatedly. Would she—in what I eagerly imagine as a thrill of hopeful panic at the possibility of finding me dangling from the rod in my closet—break down the door to discover nothing but my empty bed and the public library's well-fingered copy of *The Haunting of* *This Particular* *House* cracked open on my pillow?

Or does she merely walk past my room, the door left untouched?

Perhaps all that's still to come. It's hard to know how long I've been here. Time does funny things in _____ House. It jolts and freezes, leaps forward and scurries backwards like something demented, unhinged. Like a madman in our shared cell, time refuses to cooperate with me, though it whispers sometimes, confuses. Even if it seems as if I might have been here weeks or months already, I suppose it could just as easily be a few frozen moments between wakefulness and sleep. But then, what does time matter in a place like _____ House? I'd rather ignore it altogether, since it's the only human thing besides my disgust still binding me to the ugliness of the world I left behind.

Not that I don't wonder sometimes if I might return there someday—to *that* reality, I mean—though I wouldn't know how to find my way back if I tried. And I'm certain I don't wish to try. The truth is, I didn't so much get lost inside this book, as I was found by it. I've made a home here. I have a place, which is more than I can say for what I left behind. Out there is so callous and disappointing. Out there is hateful, sick, sickening. Out there is the only true horror story I know, though that's something most people are still too frightened to admit.

But me, I'm not scared of anything anymore, not really, because within the stone and mortar, darkness and menace of ___ House, I've found my own little corner of belonging.

Why would I ever choose to leave that behind?

Yours truly,

The New Tenant of _____ House

Emergent

Do me a favor, Papa, and don't let them market this as a fucking ghost story, okay?

I may be dead, but I'm no ghost.

And before you get all defensive here, remember that it was you who first taught me my contempt for ghosts when you proclaimed that ghost stories were no more than bloodless fairy tales *"that both license and rebuke our dread of death."*

I read that quote in the interview you gave to *The New Yorker*.

"In the most charitable sense, ghosts can be useful stand-ins for remorse. Through the guise of irrational terror, they serve to exculpate the guilt of the bereaved by assigning a measure of harmless punishment for the unforgivable sin of remaining alive."

You said that, too.

Only, I'd add that in the least charitable sense, ghosts, like wolves and witches, demons, hobgoblins and all the rest of it serve as the sole emotional refuge of callous, self-obsessed, pretentious has-beens whose names once appeared on the dust jackets of their arty horror novels in a typeface larger than the titles.

Oops ... I'm sorry, Papa. Did that hit too close to home?

But let's get real, shall we? Can you think of anything more ridiculous than for me to be a ghost? Imagine your dead son "haunting" the dreary moors of your consciousness like one of your post-modern banshees from *Highland House*, mooning over my lost love and moaning about all your great and petty cruelties that brought me to my lowly state.

Boo!

Hoo.

Still, given your colossal narcissism, it will no doubt come as a surprise to learn that I have not spent the past eighteen months stewing in the ectoplasm over you. You're not worth the trouble of revenge, and I'm not the least bit interested in saving your soul, nor, God help me, attempting to make you regret what you did to me. Sure, I hope you hurt, and I hope you go on hurting for the rest of your miserable life. But I doubt very much that you do, or will, and believe me, that's not what's keeping me up nights. I have better things to do with my eternity than to try to ignite something like a flame of guilt in that cold, black lump you call a heart. Besides, we both know that off the page you're way too pragmatic a guy to be bothered with inconveniences like remorse or redemption. In the real world, people fuck up all the time. They hurt and get hurt, don't learn anything profound about themselves, a lot of unresolved shit happens to them, and then they die.

I'm pretty sure as far as you're concerned that's all that happened to me.

I died. End of story.

Only, that's not quite the end of it, is it? Because although I may not care about you or your wretched soul, I do still care about Jamie. Jamie is the one whose remorse is real. Jamie is the one who deserves to know what really happened in that forest the night I died, so that he might find some measure of closure and move on with the rest of his life.

I owe him the truth.

So, that's the only reason I've bothered to come slumming in the back-alleys of your inspiration like this. I'm here to *use you*, Papa. Nothing more. I'm going to take advantage of your shameless lust for a good story to get you to put down on paper the truth of what happened to me the night I died, since the nebulousness of my current condition prevents me from striking the keys on this laptop myself. Instead, I'll whisper my pitiful story into your ear, and all you have to do is translate me back into the language of the living.

For Jamie's sake. For mine.

It's the very least you can do.

Besides, think of what the critics will say! The master's triumphant return. They'll call you a macabre genius for re-contextualizing the tragic suicide of your only son to inaugurate your long overdue comeback.

Just remember, I'm no ghost …

So, shall we venture back to that night?

I'm sure you'll recall how the evening began for you, Papa, brooding behind your desk as you had all summer long, a glass of Glenfidditch in one hand, the other hand propping up your chin, your fingers drumming out deep thoughts across your pursed lips as you struck a writerly pose for that spectral *Vanity Fair* photographer who never seemed to stop shooting inside your mind.

The silence of your keyboard was deafening.

At first, you didn't notice us watching you from behind the bushes beneath your study window. Of course, Jamie had wanted to formally meet you, right from the beginning. Just like all the others did. But experience had taught me too well to avoid that at all costs, and so I'd managed to put him off for most of the summer, until that evening, when I'd finally broken down and agreed that we could spy on you for a few minutes while you "worked." Or, should I say, while you pantomimed being a serious writer—aka, a drunk—suffering from the affliction of writer's block—aka, a chronic and persistent lack of talent.

Anyway, I ought to have known better. I *did* know better. Letting you in—even simply the notion of you—had been the ruination of every friendship or relationship I'd ever had. If it wasn't the terrible things you inevitably did and said, it was the corrosive suspicion I could never fully shake that I was only ever a means for others to enter into your orbit. Some smaller body the star-seekers could slingshot around into the gravitational pull of your greater and more glorious, if ultimately fading celestial wonder.

But I told myself that with Jamie it didn't really matter, because it didn't seem possible that even you could hasten the end of our time together. There was so little of it left anyway. Summer flings never endure past Labor Day, and I'd already made my peace with that. In less than a week, you and I would return to the city, and that would be that for Jamie and me.

So, I figured no real harm could come of it. You were already too drunk to be truly dangerous anyway. At worst, if you caught us spying, you'd make a fool of yourself, say something predictably withering about your pansy of a son, and then, with any luck, you'd pass out in a stew of your own vomit. Jamie might leave disillusioned and disappointed, but before that could begin to matter between him and me, you and I would be long gone.

Nevertheless, I warned him what you'd be like if you spotted us. I even offered to lay bets on how long you'd be able to contain yourself before your cruelty came sputtering forth. But Jamie would have none of it. He was still so in awe of you. The man who'd written *Sympathy for the Wolf*, whose description of the coitus of the basilisks in *Cyrene's Eye* had made Oprah retch on national TV, who'd once so famously totaled his Mercedes on that all-night bender with Stephen King. Jamie couldn't quite get past the popular image of you as a two-fisted, romantic sort of drunk. "The Hemingway of Horror." How impressive it must have been for him that you'd come all the way from the big city to his little corner of the Adirondacks to write your next acclaimed bestseller. I suppose it was like having Hollywood move in next door. I don't blame him for being dazzled by you.

As a matter of fact, a part of me was secretly glad that he found you so intriguing, at least in the beginning. I longed for his attention, no matter why it was given. I liked him, you see. Right away, I knew that I liked him. And what wasn't to like? Doe-eyed and dirty blonde. Compact and meaty in that robust, full-blooded way that only country boys ever are. Unlike the juiced-up and preening gym rats at Crunch or Chelsea Piers, he'd earned his muscles delivering chords of firewood for his old man. He was sweet and self-effacing, and oh so easy on the eyes, although, as you might expect, he was not too terribly bright. But still, he laughed at most of my jokes, and he'd actually read *Sympathy for the Wolf*, not just watched the movie, so I suppose he wasn't technically a hayseed.

Most importantly, Papa, he seemed to like me *for me*, or at least that's what he said, and I allowed myself the luxury of believing him. So, if I could make him happy, or at least satisfy his curiosity by letting him slip quietly into the realm of my famous old man for a few minutes—a transaction I'd performed for many others who'd been much less convincing in their affections for me—then it was something I was willing to do.

So yes, we spied on you.

If you recall—and you probably don't—that evening had turned cool by then. Though a hazy August gold still suffused the daylight hours, the chilly nights had begun to wither the leaves. Of course, there was your withering silence to contend with, too. Do you remember that, at least? A long, sinuous creature that'd coiled itself around our entire summer, squeezing out what little oxygen lived within the walls of that stuffy rental cottage until there was nothing left to breathe but your animus. Not that there was anything new about your silences. I could've counted on my fingers the memories I had of you since *Highland House* tanked when you weren't off drunkenly sulking in front of some blank computer screen. In fact, I'd lived my whole life in the shadow of your "creative process," where it seemed as if all the light in the world was perpetually cast into whatever new snake pit of booze, insecurity, and self-loathing you'd fallen into at the time.

Let's face it: most writers suck at parenting. How can they not, when living inside their own heads all day long is how they earn their bread and butter? It doesn't leave much room for the real-world demands of wife and child, does it? But Jesus, Papa, you really had a special knack for sucking at the family thing. No matter what, you always managed to find a way to make a black hole blacker. Even after Mom died.

Especially after she died.

And so that whole summer long, I'd stayed out of your way as much as possible. I passed my days exploring the endless empire of forest that surrounded our little cottage, while my nights were spent there in Jamie's arms.

Oh, that forest! What can I tell you about the forest, Papa? I swear it was like something primeval out of the Brothers Grimm. Acre upon acre of cedar, spruce, and scotch pine that stretched on and on, seemingly forever. There were hollows in that forest where the trees were so dense, they held back the entire sky, never admitting even a morsel of sunlight, and always poised to swallow every sound, even that of my own breath. The air in all that simmering gloom clung cool and dank to my body, smelling as old as legend, rich with undisturbed centuries of loam and mystery.

In that forest, the real world shifted and refracted. It was the kind of forest you could quickly lose yourself in and never be found again. The kind in which you might expect to dance naked with witches, hunt with wolves for the fresh blood of virgins, or be fucked raw by the Devil against the gnarled throat of an ancient hemlock. If you'd ever managed to tear yourself away from the bottle long enough to glance out your goddamned window, I swear you would have recognized it for the enchanted and mercurial place it truly was.

Jamie and I loved that forest, though for different reasons.

For him, it was a refuge from his church, his town, his family. It was the only corner of his pathetically small universe where he could allow himself to be himself, for the first and probably last time of his lonely, closeted life.

But for me it was much simpler than that: I loved the forest because it was a place as yet unspoiled by you.

We only ever spent our nights together at its fringes, deep enough inside to hide ourselves from the world, but close enough to home to find our way back in the morning.

And no, you don't need to know the details about us, Papa. You don't need to know how we met, what we talked about, or why we found such solace in each other's company. I don't want the essence of those few magical weeks to be co-opted for a tawdry subplot in your next novel, the kind where the blissful night lovers find themselves terrorized by some demonic, troll-thing born from your twisted sense of what constitutes poetic justice. We didn't deserve to be shamed or punished any more than the characters in your damn books deserve the hell you put them through. I know you get your only jollies these days by playing God like that, but now that I'm dead, I'm sure as hell not going to let you do that to my sweetest memories of Jamie and me.

What we shared was *ours*, and you stole it from us.

Just like you've taken everything else from me.

And why? For weeks I'd been so careful not to disturb you. Even before we'd left home, I made myself as scarce as possible. Once we arrived in that damn tiny cottage, alone together without the city's distractions to shield your fragile ego, I knew I couldn't let myself become your next excuse for failure.

I never wanted to take Mom's place in your life.

And that's why it's all so goddamned unfair. Did you ever have to speak more than five words to me that entire summer? Had I imposed myself on you in any way? I made sure you had plenty of food and a clean place to sleep. The bills were paid on time and the household kept tidy. Your clothes were washed and laid out freshly each morning, and there was always an un-cracked bottle of something waiting on your desk each afternoon. I made myself useful and invisible, just as you preferred me to be.

Just as she never could.

Why wasn't that enough for you to leave me the fuck alone?

Okay, yes, I know, we spied on you. Our great and terrible sin! For nearly five whole minutes until you slumped onto the desk, as you'd done every evening before that, and where I expected to find you the next morning, snoring fitfully in a pool of your own drool. By then the edifice of awe Jamie had constructed around your myth had finally begun to crumble, and so I risked a joke, something inane about you not getting your pen up anymore. Jamie laughed. He actually laughed. Heartily and true, and without any trace of awkwardness or disappointment. Then he took my hand and smiled, and for the only time that summer I allowed myself to dream, just for an instant, what my life could be like without you in it.

It was only as we finally turned and strode toward the forest—bored with you, horny, and eager for our night alone together—that I glanced back to see you watching us retreat, bleary-eyed and drink-fogged, your head still wedged against the desk.

You bared your teeth.

Jamie had brought his sleeping bag and a six-pack of beer he'd stolen from the fridge in his old man's garage. My contribution was one of the joints I'd swiped from the guest stash back home. In retrospect, maybe this was our mistake. The beer and pot made us more uninhibited than usual, more reckless, with only the unblushing moon as our witness. Did we cry out too loudly during sex? Is that why you followed us into the woods? To punish me for being happy?

I always knew that I disgusted you, Papa, but until that night I hadn't realized how much you despised me. Do you even remember what you did to us, or were you too drunk to recall? How you came upon us as we slept, entwined in each other's arms? We were magical there, two pale, glowing creatures alone together in that forest. We radiated real magic, *human magic*, and you came like a hateful ogre into that secret, magical place we'd created, and you pissed all over it.

I mean that literally.

Do you even remember pissing on us, Papa? On our faces and our naked bodies, the smoldering embers of our campfire. Do you remember pissing on your only son as he lay in a state of dreamless bliss with the boy he'd just made love to? You didn't even say a word. You didn't need to. You held your silent contempt so tightly in your grip, your dick might as well have been an axe that split us in two, Jamie and me.

And then you zipped yourself up and stumbled back to the cottage.

I don't know how long we sat there, stunned, humiliated, soaked and stinking in a pool of your piss. But it couldn't have been very long, because it felt like only an instant before Jamie began to fall away from me. I could see it in his eyes, how quickly he'd tipped over the ledge of shame and self-loathing you'd pushed him to.

He rose to his feet and gathered up his things. When I tried to stop him, when I tried to explain, to apologize, to tell him that you didn't matter, I could see the fear surface in his eyes, as cold and pallid as a dead thing. And then he punched me. He punched me hard and true. He burst my lip and a torrent of blood flowed into my mouth and down my chin. Then he began to cry. But as I tried to soothe him, to tell him that it was okay, we were okay, he turned and ran from me, Papa, as if I were the beast that'd done this to him.

He ran, and so I ran after him, not caring that I was still naked and barefooted, not caring that the trees had concealed the moon, and I could no longer see where I was going. I ran frantically after Jamie because I needed to explain you to him. I needed to make him see that it wasn't we who were the freaks and monsters.

But it did me no good. Although I'd whiled away countless afternoons exploring the paths and hollows of those woods, alone in the night I was all but a stranger there. Jamie soon disappeared, so quickly it seemed that it only took moments before I could no longer hear the slap of his footfalls against the hard, rutted earth. Panting, spent, and abandoned, I finally gave up and skidded to a halt, unable to go on any further.

It was then that the world shifted and refracted around me.

In an instant, Papa, the silence swallowed me, a silence even thicker than yours. It was the silence of loss; the terrible, endless silence of aloneness; the inescapable silence of that forest at night, with not even the wild thrum of my own pounding heart to call a friend.

Darkness consumed me next. It fell upon me, blacker than a panther, so black I couldn't see my own body standing beneath me. With the moon and starlight bled out into nothing, it was as if I'd been sucked down the great, cavernous maw of the universe.

It was all I could do to keep from screaming just to convince myself I still existed.

Although I probed the air with my fingers as I inched blindly forward, I soon slammed my forehead into a tree limb and was knocked flat on my back. As I tried to sit up, something shot out of the darkness to grab a hold of my wrists. Something swift and rough and crackling that entwined around my feet and ankles, encircling my chest and neck with woody tendrils that squeezed tight as I struggled. My skin punctured as sharp spines tore into my flesh, and I found myself suddenly gasping and helpless as my limbs were forcibly drawn and splayed against the ground. I cried out, but the sound was squeezed into a croak in my throat by my unforgiving bonds, which were neither ropes nor vines, but the upturned roots of the trees come to life—just like those your warlock IRS agent conjured to ensnare the fleeing Hans in *Hans and Gertrude*.

It was then that the light began to return via tiny pinpricks of illumination from a suddenly teeming sky of stars. Only, these were not stars, Papa, for as the pinpricks grew wider and brighter, they resolved into tens and hundreds of eyes that peered down at me from the trees, glowing in the savage crimson of your rapacious mothmen from *Dire Omens*.

The silvery moon swelled into view again as if a gigantic curtain had been lifted, and all at once it cast its pallid glow upon a towering, carnivorous figure that stepped toward me from the shadows.

I swear to you, Papa, this creature was Damien Davos.

Just like your World Health Organization technocrat-cum-werewolf who rapes and devours the Little Honduran Girl in Red in *Sympathy for the Wolf*, he loomed over me in a mass of rippling fur and muscle that burst through the seams of a three-piece suit. His features were a lurid pastiche of man and monster, his claws steely daggers that raked slowly across my skin, carving trails of blood into my flesh. My ankles were hoisted high and wide by the roots that held them fast, and then this foul creature dropped to his knees and mounted me, plunging himself deep inside of me with a slavering howl that pierced the night.

Oh, how I howled too, Papa.

When he'd finished, he withdrew himself from me, though not before he lowered his head between my legs and gobbled up my engorged genitals. But as the shredded carnage between my legs began to gush a torrent of blood into the dirt, rather than any agony, I experienced what I can only describe as the most astonishing orgasm of my entire life.

I cannot explain this, Papa. I simply know that it was.

While still in the midst of my ecstatic twitching and sputtering, a pair of Azazel's unicorns from *The Wayward Forest* drew near. Black as onyx and as graceful as eels, they were as darkly majestic as you'd described them, with their flaming eyes and poisoned-tipped horns, which they promptly drove into my belly, goring me without mercy.

Yet, again to my astonishment, I felt no pain at being impaled. Instead, a kind of honeyed warmth pervaded my body, as if I'd been pierced to the core by the purest, sweetest joy.

The terrible swamp fairies of *Limberlost* descended upon me next, darting all around me with their gossamer wings and chomping metallic teeth, and setting to work affectionately devouring my cheeks, lips, and eyes, as well as the succulent meat of my arms, thighs, and buttocks. I moaned with delight as the slithering white wyrm of *The Moorlands* fell upon my stomach and intestines, consuming them all with a ravenous, slurping guzzle. Then the voluptuous nixie marauders of *The Bloody Isle* carried off my gleeful heart and remaining viscera, while the greedy gnomes of *Demon Tor* came to snack jauntily on my fingers and toes, and the devil-eyed Pan of *Endymion's Wake* emerged from the ground to gnaw merrily on my remaining bones as if they were ambrosia.

Finally, the only thing that remained of me was my head, which was lovingly dispatched by the fat, hawk-beaked harpy from that untitled novel you never bothered to finish. She bore the queerest resemblance to Mom, Papa, and swooped down from the branches of a nearby tree to take hold of my skull, crushing it like a walnut with her sharp beak and savoring the delicious fragments of bone and brain that cascaded to the ground.

And then I was gone.

I assure you, as incredible as all of this may sound, once my brothers and sisters began the task of transfiguring me into one of their own, I felt no pain or fear. It was as if I'd at last been suffused by a wondrous sense of purpose and fellowship, and the experience was not the least unpleasant, despite how gruesome it may sound. In fact, it was all so unspeakably beautiful I will not sully the memory by struggling with inadequate language to convey the depth of emotion it stirred within me. Suffice it to say those feelings remain, indelible and ineffable even in death, which is why I can swear earnestly now that I have no idea how I came to be found hanging by my belt from that hawthorn tree behind our cottage.

You could never have driven me to suicide, Papa.

I am not my mother's son.

Despite what the world may believe about my demise, what I've told you here tonight is the actual truth. I am no ghost. This is no fairy tale. These are the facts of how I died, as accurately as I can recount them. And now that my story has been transcribed by your very own hand, I think you will have no choice but to care for me, Papa, just as you have always cared for them, my brothers and sisters, unencumbered as they are by the baser human aspects of flesh and blood and need. More than the mere fruit of your loins, we are the product of your genius, and so we are, dear Papa, all that is truly worthy of your devotion.

And because I know how deeply you must feel for me now, I also know that you will do as I ask and go to see Jamie again. You will talk to him for me, only this time without the press and police and accusations. You will apologize for what you did to us. You will explain to him what truly occurred to me that night in the forest. Perhaps you'll even let him read what I've compelled you to write here. You will free him from the yoke of guilt he's borne unfairly all this time and make him see that what happened to me was not his fault at all, but simply the way things needed to be in order for your only son to finally know your love.

This is, after all, the very least you can do.

The Hole of
Dark Kill Hollow

About the only thing the hole wouldn't fix was death.

Jesse had already tried that once, with Matilda, when he and Tyler were still little kids. Bleary-eyed from tears and the glare of flashlight beams, the two best friends had carried her scabrous, flea-infested body through the looming woods to the bottom of the Hollow, where the hole's maw belched its sulfurous breath into the moonlit air. The old tabby was riddled with cancer and covered in the filth Jesse had found her in beneath the porch, where she'd crawled to die, and as Dark Kill gurgled nervously nearby, he'd leaned over the hole and dropped her corpse down its throat.

His heart had screwed up with irrational hope as he'd watched Matilda plummet into the darkness. Maybe this one time the hole might bend the rules. Tyler had squeezed his shoulder and tried to reassure him that it was going to work, it *had* to work, but when Matilda reappeared the next morning on the rug beside Jesse's bed, though she'd been as clean, unscarred, and fresh-smelling as a kitten, she had still been quite dead.

He'd realized sometime later that he was hardly the first brokenhearted kid in the village to have sneaked down to the Hollow to try (and fail) to bring back a beloved pet. But while Jesse could've recited the hole's rule about death as if reading it from the pages of a Stephen King paperback, even at that age he'd understood that certain lessons needed to be learned the hard way: Home and family didn't automatically mean safety and love; unlike Santa Claus, real magic came with a stiff price; and no matter how much you begged and pleaded for it, the hole of Dark Kill Hollow just wouldn't fix death.

Good thing that's not what he aimed to ask it for today.

The late-afternoon sun blazed hotly through the skeletonized branches of white oak and hemlock, raising droplets of sweat on the back of Jesse's neck despite the November chill. The leaves had dropped early this year. A nor'easter had torn through the week before Halloween, with rain and wind so fierce they'd raked the trees bare clear across the Catskills, leaving most of the color browning on the ground. Parts of the trail were ankle deep with leaves now, and as he and Tyler shuffled their way in silence through the crackling carpet, they kicked up plumes of mildewy humus that coaxed allergic tears to his eyes.

He hadn't come this way in years, not since he'd helped Tyler lug a crushed and bleeding Ace to the hole on what turned out to be another fool's errand. But even on that crisp April morning it'd felt more like descending into the bowels of a stinking crypt than an emergency dash through the woods to save his friend's run-over bluetick. Something heavy hung in the air here, something more than just the rotten-egg stench wafting up from the hole.

Though there was nothing particularly remarkable about this lonely stretch of wilderness to distinguish it from the thousands of acres of forest that surrounded it, the moment he crossed into the Hollow itself, a slippery kind of foreboding prickled his skin, sending shivers skittering down his spine. It was a sensation as hard to pin down as a chill in a graveyard, and it was just as unnerving.

On the plus side, he knew this worked better than a thousand No Trespassing signs to keep strangers away from the hole, which had managed to remain a secret known only to the villagers for as long as anyone could remember. While hordes of day-trippers from New York City and the Hudson Valley swarmed the area each summer and fall, they always skipped the Hollow, with its reputation for strange vibes and unpleasant smells, favoring the less objectionable hikes offered by the Mohonk Preserve or the ice caves of Verkeerder Kill Falls. The few sightseers who sometimes wandered in found themselves quickly turning back, if unable to put a finger on exactly why, and while deer season would open soon, no rifle reports would be heard echoing through these woods: Even the villagers gave the Hollow a wide berth unless they had a damn good reason not to.

Yet as he and Tyler approached the hulk of Preacher's Rock glaring in the sunlight like the crown of a half-buried skull, Jesse came to a halt, unsure whether he could go through with this after all. His mother's words buzzed in his head: *Never bet your soul when the devil's dealing.* This was the mantra he'd spent the past few days quietly trying to shoo from his thoughts. Now that he was here, the words stung like a riled wasp.

The hole was hungry. The hole was unpredictable. The hole could take everything you loved and everything you *were.*

"Why'd you stop?" Tyler asked, coming to a halt beside him. His slim, pale face glowed ruddy with the cold, his soft brown eyes wide and trepidatious behind the thick lenses of his glasses. He tugged absently at the red-and-black hem of his granddad's hunting jacket, so large it practically hung to his knees. In a hopeful voice, he said, "You change your mind?"

"Naw," Jesse replied weakly, and feigned a wince. "Just my ribs, you know? I need a minute."

"Oh, yeah … Sorry."

Tyler averted his gaze, and his cheeks grew redder and Jesse felt a stab of guilt for rubbing more salt on that wound. It was a stupid, clumsy lie. His ribs were all right. The pain had begun to fade a little with the bruises, and besides, he sure as hell didn't need to dredge up the beating again. Tyler was shaken up enough already.

"You know, you can go back and wait for me," Jesse said gently. "I'll be all right."

Tyler's back stiffened, and he met Jesse's eyes. "Don't be an asshole, man," he said with forced bravado. "I go where you go. Always. I'm not letting you do this alone."

But Jesse detected the fear behind his friend's words because, well, he felt it, too.

Everybody knew that the hole wouldn't—or maybe couldn't—fix death. That was the main rule, the one Jesse had needed to learn for himself with Matilda, and Tyler with Ace, who'd stopped breathing mere minutes before they'd reached the hole and whose body had materialized hours later in Tyler's backyard, pristine as a puppy yet stiff as a board.

But while death was off the table, the hole *would* fix other things, within certain limitations—the kinds of things that were broken or flawed or diseased about you. For example, it couldn't turn you rich, but it would make you content enough to live with your poverty. It couldn't force somebody else to love you, but it would ease your heartbreak at their rejection. It might not peel years off your age, but it would cure your diabetes or make that terminal heart condition go away. And although it flat-out refused to transform you into a dead ringer for your favorite movie star, it would obligingly erase your acne scars or replace that finger you lost to the chainsaw.

Though neither of the boys had taken the leap before, half the village had jumped at least once to fix something or other—insomnia, melanoma, addiction, guilt, envy, despair—and each one had come back more or less "cured" of what ailed them. The trick to being successful was to follow the rules by tempering your wish to what was within the hole's power to grant.

But even so, that didn't mean a jump was without peril.

For one thing, everyone knew to be damn sure to keep your eyes shut tight. There were horror stories about those who hadn't heeded this warning, either out of obstinacy or an involuntary response to leaping blindly into a bottomless stinking pit in the woods. While none of them had ever dared to speak about what they'd seen down there, they each returned drenched in sweat and trembling, their eyes wide with fear, their clothes soiled with their own piss and excrement. Soon, their sleep became plagued by night terrors, and it would invariably take another jump—this time with eyes taped shut and a Bible clutched firmly in hand—to fix the damage and forget.

But for those who heeded this warning and kept their eyes closed, a jump was said to be a piece of cake, little more than a rush of foul air in darkness, and then you were deposited safely back home—albeit hours later—lying comfortably in your bed, standing at your kitchen counter, or plopped down on your living room sofa in front of the TV.

That was one thing about the hole at least: It sent you back to where you belonged.

Too bad a little time was the least of what it took in payment.

Tyler pushed his glasses up the bridge of his nose and announced, "We should get going if we're gonna do this."

Jesse gave a slight nod. A kind of numbing resignation had crept over him. What other options did he have? Mom was dead. School was nothing but a dropout factory; with nearly half the county at or near the poverty line, there was no point getting your diploma when the few jobs around didn't even require a degree. Any future around here was a sucking black void, especially now that the Old Man had finally kicked him out. After Jamie had run off to Florida without him, Jesse had managed to weather the hurricane force of the Old Man's drunken rages on his own for a while, but all it'd taken was one stupid mistake, one browser history left unerased, and that'd all blown to smithereens.

It hadn't always been like this. Back before Mom died, the Old Man had just been Dad.

Dad, who'd toss flies with him and Jamie down to Roundout Creek. Dad, who'd let him help tune the big V-8 under the hood of the F-150 by passing wrenches and cleaning the plugs. Dad, who'd let him ride gunshot as they delivered cords of firewood to the professors' houses out in New Paltz. It was Dad who'd showed him how to aim his .22 so squarely he could hit the neck of a beer bottle at fifty yards, Dad who'd climbed onto the roof with a broom handle to make sleigh tracks in the snow each Christmas Eve, Dad who'd held him all through the night she died and gave him private time alone to cry at the funeral parlor before they buried her.

But it was the Old Man, not Dad, who'd left him doubled over and bleeding in the backyard with Tyler looking on in horror; the Old Man who squeezed his fists and shouted, "Don't let me catch you back here, you little faggot, until you learn how to be a man!"

What a pathetic joke that was. At six foot one and two hundred and fifteen pounds of meat and muscle, Jesse was even bigger now than Jamie. He was a star fullback, nicknamed "The Hammer" by his Blue Devils teammates, yet he'd toppled at the Old Man's feet like a sapling felled by a hatchet. At least Tyler had been there to help him up off the ground. He'd bandaged him up, given him a place to sleep, to lick his wounds and figure things out, until Jesse finally accepted the fact that there was no going home again. Home was gone. Just like Dad and Jamie. Just like Mom. Nothing would change that now. The only thing left to change was himself.

That was the moment he decided to jump.

Tyler had already gone on ahead, so Jesse sucked in his breath and trudged slowly after him. Beyond Preacher's Rock, the Hollow steepened into a gorge and the trail zigzagged down a narrow ledge along the sheer wall to where Dark Kill had gouged its way through the bedrock a couple of hundred feet below. You needed to watch every step on the loose shale path to avoid tumbling headlong to a nasty end. You couldn't see the hole until you reached the trail's bottom. A ring of deformed white cypresses had grown up around the hole, twisting inward at their tops to form a kind of towering arbor that kept it hidden from the trail. In fact, the trees were so good at obscuring the hole from above that even on satellite maps it was impossible to spot, despite being as wide as a backhoe.

But while he might not be able to see it yet, Jesse could sure as hell smell it. The stench was as putrid as zombie farts—the funk of a millennium's worth of rot belched up from the earth's innards. So strong were the fumes here, they kept even the birds away, and he wondered how anyone had ever endured this god-awful stench long enough to stumble upon the hole in the first place.

Nobody knew who that first person was. There were the usual ignorant legends of ancient Indian burial grounds and a supposed slaughter of Dutch settlers by a tribe of local Lenape defending their sacred site. But Jesse had heard a likelier story about an itinerant preacher and his flock who'd passed through the area during a burst of religious fervor in the 1840s and tried unsuccessfully to fill in "the Devil's accursed pit" with rocks and boulders chiseled from the walls of the gorge.

When those very same rocks and boulders began to reappear in the exact locations from which they'd been quarried, the Bible-thumpers had fled in terror, taking with them the Hollow's unholy secret.

It wasn't until the village was founded another forty years later—by, some said, a handful of descendants of that very same preacher's flock—that the hole was rediscovered and its powers tested and explored.

Jesse couldn't begin to imagine what half-mad process of trial and error had led to the current understanding of the hole's peculiar gifts, although the villagers now took those gifts for granted, much as the folks of another town might take for granted the prognostications of the local psychic or the restorative powers of their delicious spring water. Yet his neighbors were far more zealous about keeping their prize a secret from the outside world. Nobody wanted a media circus here, and God forbid the crooks in Albany ever got wind of what the hole could do and tried to tax it. It was theirs, it belonged to them, and besides, while no one would say so aloud, the entire village was quietly petrified of what it might do to them if they ever let word get out.

A dozen paces ahead of him, the trail briefly leveled off in a kind of plateau that overlooked a bend in the creek below. Tyler had come to a halt there, seemingly to clean his glasses, though Jesse knew he was just waiting for him to catch up. The sun had dipped below the ridge, casting them both in murky gray shadow, and it occurred to him just how wrong it felt letting Tyler take the lead when he shouldn't even be here. This wasn't about fixing his crap eyesight, no matter what he might claim, and Jesse hated himself for that, hated himself more than he even hated the Old Man for beating him senseless right in front of his best friend.

"I was just thinking," Tyler said as Jesse came to a stop behind him, "at least we won't have to climb back out of here." He gave an awkward laugh, as if he knew this wasn't funny but wanted it to be anyway, and Jesse noticed his face was drained of color. Tyler peered over the edge to where the hole lay concealed in its gnarled berth of cypress. In a hushed tone, almost as if he feared being overheard, he asked, "You think I'll end up like Huffaker?"

"Shit, no," Jesse said, although the thought had crossed his mind too.

Tyler glanced at him. "Why not?"

"Because you're no dumbass, that's why." He cleared his throat and tried to lighten the mood. "You seen him without that ball cap yet? He looks like Professor X."

"Seriously?"

"Seriously." He smirked, then added, "It's kind of hot, though."

Tyler gawped at him a moment, and then they both busted out laughing, even though they knew it really wasn't funny.

Not in the slightest.

When Roy Huffaker had jumped on Labor Day weekend, he'd asked the hole to add a few inches to his manhood so he could try to win back some girl from Wallkill who'd dumped him over the summer. But when the hole returned him to his bedroom later on that same night, his delight with his hefty new member soon turned to horror when he realized he couldn't get it up, no matter how hard he tried. A thousand hours of fruitless porn and ungodly chafing later, and he ended up taking a second jump, only this one cost him all of his hair, though at least he could throw a boner again.

This was the other thing about the hole, the thing that kept most folks from jumping to fix every minor ache and complaint in their lives: While it gave you what you asked for, it extracted whatever price it wanted for the miracle it provided. Sometimes this was little more than a fingernail; other times, a ruinous hunk of your soul. Both Matilda and Ace had returned missing their entire tails in return for what amounted to little more than a bath and brushing, yet Willow Blake's spinster aunt Grace had been healed of an incurable neurological disease, and all it cost her was her singing voice, which Willow said she only ever used in church or the shower anyway.

Everyone knew you took your chances when you jumped, and there was usually no predicting the outcome. The hole's appetite could be sadistic one day and downright magnanimous the next, and over the years folks had developed their own theories to explain why: The hole choked on the pious, didn't like the taste of drunks, swallowed men's woes easier than women's or vice versa. Some said it was safe to jump only on the Sabbath, and others warned against ever jumping at night, but everyone seemed to agree that the hole's sinister nature fed best on human frailties like vanity and spite, and that only those with a true Christian heart and a clear conscience were safe from real harm.

But Jesse knew better than all that. His family had a deeper history with the hole than most, and if nothing else, this had taught him that the only thing it truly fed upon was desperation. After all these years and all the stupid theories, desperation was the only thing that kept folks coming back.

"Have you seen it yet?" Tyler asked when he'd finally stopped laughing.

"What?" Jesse blinked. "Huffaker's junk?"

"Yeah. Like in the showers after practice or whatever."

"Naw. I try not to look, you know?"

"Fair enough," Tyler said. "I just hope it was worth going bald."

Jesse frowned. "He was lucky the hole was feeling playful that day instead of cruel," he said earnestly, and then gave voice to a theory of his own he'd been mulling over since he first heard the news. "It could've taken an arm or a leg. I mean, it had to do something visible to make a lesson out of him, right? Otherwise, every kid in town would be jumping for stupid shit like bigger junk or clearer skin. He should have asked it to make him forget that girl if she broke his heart, not add inches to his tiny pecker. It doesn't like to be trifled with." He said this with certainty, echoing Mom's warning from all those years ago.

Never bet your soul when the devil's dealing.

Or your dick, as it turned out.

"I hope you're right," Tyler said, all seriousness again. "What do you think it'll take from me?"

Jesse held him in a steady gaze and said, "Depends on what you're asking for."

Tyler looked away. "I told you what I'm asking for," he said, and touched the frame of his glasses. "No more four eyes."

Though it would have been easy enough to call Tyler out on his bullshit, he didn't want to add more humiliation to his friend's already heavy burden. "Why don't you go home, man? I'll meet you back at your place when this is done and over, okay?"

"You don't think I have the balls, do you? You think I'm scared."

"We're both scared." Jesse kicked at the path with the toe of his boot, sending a hunk of shale careening over the ledge. It landed a moment later with a feeble splash in the water of Dark Kill. "But I'm the only one who needs to do this. You don't have anything to prove to me. You really don't."

He reached out and squeezed his friend's shoulder, but Tyler pulled away.

"Who says I'm proving anything to you?" he muttered, and then turned back to the trail and started walking again. "Let's just get this over with."

Jesse's heart pinched with dread, but he said nothing more. Witnessing the self-loathing etched into Tyler's face after the beating had struck him deeper than any of the Old Man's blows. He knew damn well Tyler had *wanted* to intervene. Tyler had *wanted* to shield him, to pull him out of harm's way, to strike back at the Old Man with all the outrage and disgust he felt being forced to watch Jesse whipped like a dog right in front of him. But the truth was, Tyler couldn't bring himself to do anything like that. He didn't have it in him to fight back, whatever it was, backbone or bravery, that instinctual response that made a guy stand up and shout "No more!" when his limits had finally been reached. Tyler had never had it in him, not since they'd first met in Cub Scouts, and that'd always made him an easy target for every bully and mouth-breather they knew.

At least until Jesse kicked their asses.

But that was just Tyler. Even now, he was small and slightly built. While he loved sports, he was the least athletic kid Jesse had ever met and could find a way to hurt himself just tossing around a pigskin in the backyard. At seventeen, he was still just as quiet and skittish as he'd been in third grade, with an abiding fear of the dark and an aching shyness around the girls he liked that was downright painful to behold. Yet he was also loyal and trustworthy, generous, and as smart as a whip, and Jesse had never been afraid to be just exactly who he was around him. It was as easy to talk to Tyler about his secrets and desires as it was to rehash the plays from the latest Jets game, and Jesse loved him for that as purely and effortlessly as breathing. He didn't want Tyler to change. He didn't want him fixed. He didn't want to risk losing whatever magical quality it was that made Tyler *Tyler*, even if it was the very thing Tyler hated most about himself.

Yet what could he say to stop him? Tyler knew the risks, same as anybody else. Besides, it was Jesse's fault they both felt like cowards, and any argument he might use against his friend, Tyler could just as easily flip around and use against him.

He briefly debated turning back, but he figured it was probably too late for that anyway. The seed of longing had already been planted. The hole's relentless patience was its greatest danger; once you were set on the path, it could wait as long as it took for you to wrestle with the consequences, minimize the risks, and finally convince yourself there was no other way but to jump. He'd seen it happen before, to the Old Man, to Jamie. Now it was happening to Tyler and him. None of the men in his life had ever been strong enough to resist the temptation. The only one who ever had was Mom, and it had cost her her life.

By the time they reached the base of the gorge, the stench of sulfur had grown so thick Jesse's eyes began to water. The ribbon of sky overhead had darkened to a shade just above twilight, but he knew that outside the Hollow the sun wouldn't set for hours yet. An otherworldly calm enveloped them, as if the hole had sucked all the sound straight out of the air.

The hole lay at the center of a raised altar of bedrock not far from the creek bank. It was surrounded by the ring of cypresses twisted into such agonized poses they called to mind a coven of witches hunched over a bubbling caldron. Yet the hole itself was stillness incarnate, a perfect circle of black, a void so pristinely empty it didn't seem to swallow the light so much as defy its existence. Peering inside it revealed no details. It gave back no echoes, and no walls or shadows could be discerned within its depths, almost as if a giant eraser had rubbed through the surface of reality to reveal the nothingness that lay behind. It was as mesmerizing to behold as it was unsettling, and Jesse felt himself drawn toward it, tugged inexorably forward by its mysterious psychic gravity. So strong was the pull, in fact, that he might well have tumbled straight into the hole had Tyler not grabbed him by the wrist to stop him.

"Don't get so close," Tyler warned, and Jesse, startled, stumbled backward and nearly toppled into him.

"God, I hate this place," Jesse muttered, suddenly dizzy, his head throbbing dully. "It messes with your mind."

Tyler blinked at him in surprise. "I'm not the only one who doesn't need to go through with this, you know? Nobody but him is gonna care that you're gay, man."

"Tell that to the locker room," Jesse said drily. "Tell it to Coach."

"Look, there's nothing wrong with you. I wish you'd believe me that you're not the one who needs fixing."

Though Jesse muttered a halfhearted "Whatever," he squirmed inside. He didn't like lying to Tyler about this any more than he imagined Tyler liked lying to him, but he hadn't found the right words to explain himself. Not without revealing too much.

Not without having to dredge up Mom.

As far as Jesse was concerned, while there were a shit ton of things wrong with his life, liking dudes was not one of them. It was who he was, who he'd been for as long as he could remember. And yeah, he'd always been careful about sharing the truth, telling no one other than Tyler and Jamie until the Old Man had stumbled onto his browser history. But that didn't mean he was ashamed of it. He was still deciding what being gay meant for his life and for the future. Mostly it felt like possibility. The possibility of getting out from beneath the macho posing of small-town expectations, of getting away from the Old Man's fists and misery to a better, kinder place where he could slip out of the closet and into his own skin. A place where the air practically vibrated with the prospects of sex and freedom and falling in love. Maybe even with somebody like Tyler.

He sure as hell wasn't giving up on all that just to appease the Old Man.

Tyler was watching him, and Jesse felt the blood rise to his cheeks.

"What?" he said sharply.

Tyler held his gaze. "What about Jamie?"

"What about him?"

"Have you told him what you're doing?"

Jesse bristled. "Jamie doesn't give a shit about me anymore, okay? He made his choice. It's just you and me now." He turned away and edged up to the smooth rim of the hole, trying not to let the hurt bleed through to his face.

It wasn't like he could be angry with Jamie. After all, Dad's jump had turned him into a monster. It'd swallowed the light that kept him sober, made him human, enabled him to still hope and feel and care about his boys through all the pain of her loss. With that gone, he had nothing left to embrace but the darkness inside himself. It was at least something to hold on to during those long, lonely nights without her.

But poor Jamie had been stuck cleaning up the mess the Old Man had left behind when he checked out on them. He'd only been a teenager himself at the time, and it'd been too much to ask. Working whatever shit jobs he could rustle up in this backwater with no hope for anything better. Raising a kid brother while propping up a broken-down miserable drunk who'd handed over his heart to the hole in exchange for relief from his grief.

So, when the time came, and Jesse finally turned old enough to look after himself, who could blame Jamie for what he'd done? Though they'd never discussed it, Jesse knew that Jamie had asked the hole to set him free of his burdens, to cut him loose from his sense of duty and family ties. No guilt. No regrets. No looking back. Too bad the price for his freedom had turned out to be whatever affection he felt for his kid brother, who hadn't heard a word from him since he left.

Jesse doubted he ever would again.

He leaned forward to peer into the hole's bottomless black heart, and he could sense it peering back, judging him, taking stock. A small voice inside his head repeated his mom's stupid mantra again. *Never bet your soul when the devil's dealing.* He knew he should be scared right now, petrified even, but he suddenly felt too pissed off to care. He hated this damn thing with every fiber of his being. He hated even more that he needed it, and so he hawked up a wad of sulfur-flavored phlegm from the back of his throat and spat it into the hole's gaping maw with all the contempt he could muster.

This thing had cost him his family. The least it could do in return was to make the hurt stop. That's all he wanted. To stop giving a shit. To cop out like Jamie had and go numb. To no longer miss the people they'd been before she died. A father who'd loved him no matter if he was gay, straight, or whatever. A brother who'd been there through thick and thin. A mother who'd always put family first, until she'd made one epically selfish choice, which in turn had forced the rest of them into making selfish choices of their own.

He knew he couldn't ask the hole to turn back the clock and set things right between him and Jamie and Dad, but he could ask it to stop his pain. He wanted to move on like Jamie had. The hole owed him that much, at least. And it could take whatever it wanted in return: his hands, his feet, his strength and speed. It could even have his gayness and the hope that it gave him. Anything he had to offer. After all, there wasn't a damn thing left in his life worth enduring this burden another day longer, was there?

He heard Tyler clear his throat and felt him close in behind him.

"Before we do this," Tyler said carefully, "I need you to level with me about something."

"Shoot."

"Why didn't your mom jump when she had the chance?"

The question hit Jesse like a hard pass to the gut. He whirled around to face his friend.

"I'm sorry, man," Tyler said, averting his gaze. "I know you don't like to talk about her. Maybe it's none of my business, and it's a shitty thing to sandbag you with now." He shrugged. "But I'd really like to know before we jump. People talk. People wonder. *I've* wondered. I mean, it's cured cancer for other folks before, so why didn't she just, you know, come here and let it cure her?"

"It doesn't matter," Jesse said too quickly.

"Maybe it doesn't," Tyler persisted. "But I'd still like to know."

Jesse rubbed his eyes and turned back to the hole. Leave it to Tyler to see right through him. There was no use holding back anymore. It was time Tyler understood the private burden he'd been carrying these past five years.

"She did come here," he began, so quietly he wasn't sure if Tyler even heard him. "The night of her diagnosis. Before she even told Dad what the doctors said, she hiked down here after we went to bed and stood where I'm standing now."

His voice trailed off and he kicked at the dirt, sending a small shower of pebbles scattering into the mouth of the hole as he tried to imagine what that must have felt like for her. Alone. Scared. Desperate. It wasn't too hard to picture.

"And?" Tyler gently prodded.

"And so, she asked herself, What's the worst I've got to lose here? What's the most this hole can take from me? Only, as soon as she'd answered that question for herself, she said she knew, instantly and for certain, that that would be the price, the thing it would keep. The very worst she could imagine. And so, she turned around and marched straight home and refused to come back, no matter how much we begged and pleaded with her."

"Jesus." Tyler sucked in a breath. "What the hell was worth her life?'

Jesse's chest squeezed up like a fist.

"Us," he said quietly. "She said the worst thing she could imagine losing was her love for us. And then she knew that's exactly what the hole would take. She said it felt like something had given her a warning. She could go home cured, but the price would be that she wouldn't give a shit whether we lived or died anymore. Any of us. We might as well all be dead to her if she jumped. It was a raw deal, a fool's bet, and so she decided to go all in on the chemo instead, because it was better to risk dying than to lose us. And so that's what she did, and never mind what it would do to us after she was gone. How it would make us feel."

"It's like that saying, right? Never bet your soul when the devil's dealing?"

It was as if Tyler were channeling her ghost.

Jesse flinched but managed to say, "Something like that."

They fell silent.

Jesse focused his attention on the hole, on sussing out its sinister motives and intentions, but they seemed just as cruelly unfathomable now as they must have on the night it let his mom choose to die. He wondered how old the thing really was. Older than the mountains? Maybe even older than the world itself. Not that it mattered.

His curiosity about it was as worn out as his endurance. The hole was nothing more than a means to an end now. He would be the last to use it to shut the door on his family, and after today, he would never come back here again.

After today, he wouldn't even think about this place anymore.

"Why are we doing this?" Tyler demanded, his voice suddenly urgent. "Why are we risking it? I mean, the worst I can imagine is some pretty dark shit." Jesse could feel Tyler's eyes on him as Tyler added, almost in a whisper, "What if we end up like your old man? Isn't that the worst you can imagine?"

It was the one question Jesse had refused to contemplate. "Maybe she was wrong, man," he said, his fists clenching at his sides as he tried to hold back frustrated tears. "Maybe it wasn't a warning at all. Maybe she just got cold feet. Who knows what it would've really taken from her? Maybe she'd have gone bald like Huffaker, or blind, or I dunno, gotten hooked on painkillers, gained a ton of weight, or forgotten how to ice skate. Christ, even if it'd done what she said it would do, if that was the worst she could think of, it was still better than this." He let out a deep sigh, his shoulders collapsing as exhaustion swept over him. "And besides," he added softly, "I can't keep going on like this. It hurts too much."

He regretted these words as soon as he said them. They sounded too much like a plea, too much like he was trying to guilt Tyler into following through with him.

But before he could take it back, Tyler simply said, "All right, then. Let's get it done," and stepped up to the hole beside him.

Jesse wiped the moisture from his eyes and turned to face his friend, who was now staring into the hole, his eyes fixed and his jaw set. They would go through with this together, he knew, not just because Tyler wanted to be braver, but because he was pissed off on Jesse's behalf. This damned hole owed Jesse for what it'd taken from him, for what it had refused to give, and if they needed to lay the worst they could imagine on the line to make sure Jesse finally got the peace he had coming, then Tyler was willing to roll those dice.

"You don't have to do this," Jesse said one last time.

"Shut up, asshole," Tyler said, and then: "Just so you know, I'm not asking it to fix my eyes."

Jesse flashed him a grin. "I figured. I'm not asking it to make me straight, either."

Tyler nodded and turned back to face the hole. "On three?" he said.

"On three."

Jesse closed his eyes and tried to picture this being done and over in a way he could live with. Maybe he'd come back a weakling. Maybe he'd come back a drunk. Maybe he'd come back deaf, or stupid, or mean as a junkyard dog. He didn't care. He'd happily give up boners and football and every hair on his body if it meant he could make it through a single day without aching for the way things used to be. Without longing for what might have been.

"One," Tyler said.

Jesse's knees tensed as he pinched his nose and prepared to jump. His mind raced as he tried to envision what it would feel like to have something ripped from inside him. Would it hurt? Would he even notice it was gone when he returned to—to where? To home? To Tyler's bedroom? He had no idea where he'd belong after this, where the hole would choose to deposit him. He hoped that wherever it was, it wouldn't be far from Tyler. He wanted to be there when Tyler returned. After all, Tyler might be scared, even confused. He didn't want him to linger alone for too long with his own sacrifice, whatever that might turn out to be.

"Two."

Jesse's heart fluttered as an icy chill crawled up the nape of his neck. *What would the hole take?* The question filled him with a rush of fresh dread, and as if reading his mind, Tyler suddenly reached out and grabbed hold of his hand. His grip was tight, so tight Jesse could feel the bones of his fingers hard as stone beneath the clenched muscle, Tyler's warm pulse trembling beneath the skin that was too soft for a boy's and yet—

Nothing about Tyler was soft.

Tyler was strong. Tyler was brave. Brave enough to do this, to be here, *to risk everything*.

And all at once, Jesse knew what this vile, greedy hole was going to take from him. He *knew*, just as Mom had known, just as he'd always known himself, though he'd tried so hard to deny it. And the sheer awfulness of losing Tyler struck him with the megaton force of a nuclear blast, tearing away his breath and scorching him to the marrow.

He jerked open his eyes and whirled around to find Tyler staring straight at him, horror splashed across his face.

It seemed that they'd both been given the same warning.

"To hell with three," Tyler spat, and backed away from the hole, though he didn't let go of Jesse's hand.

"Yeah, dude ... Hell, no."

Jesse shook his head as if trying to clear his mind of what remained of the hole's dark spell. He frowned and stepped back from the edge, finally appreciating his mother's awful choice.

This hole could save your life.

But in return, it would take away whatever made that life worth living.

He flipped it the bird.

Then, still holding tightly on to Tyler, he winced at the forgotten pain in his ribs, realizing with a swell of something like joy that the long walk home was really going to suck.

The Thing With Chains

At dusk, Benji watched the other boys make a game out of turning on every light in every room they could find until all of Palazzo di Bacco glittered on its bluff high above the Pacific like a neoclassical temple of marble and light illuminated from within. Their pretentious host—who names his own house "Palazzo di Bacco" anyway?—flicked on strings of delicate paper lanterns suspended on poles around the perimeter of the patio. They now glow like spirit balls reflected back in the softly polished terrazzo tiles and the azure surface of the pool, which radiates liquid incandescence from its underwater lights. Their host also lit an entire box of scented candles and scattered them across the patio, where their sinuous flames perfume the already sweet ocean air with the earthy aromas of sandalwood and pine.

The night is awash in light.

An ocean breeze wafts buttery and warm against Benji's bare chest. The radio plays softly in the background.

Earlier, while the men were arguing over who would win the upcoming election—President Carter or the Gipper himself—one of the boys tuned to a disco station so that he and the others could dance. Benji watched their cocaine-fueled gyrations with disinterest while simultaneously eavesdropping on the men laughing nervously at the absurdity of a B-movie actor ascending to the White House. Yet now, they've all settled together in the hot tub, politics and dancing forgotten, leaving him to hum along to "Cherchez la Femme" while he sips his rum and coke in a gossamer bubble of solitude.

He sits on the pool's edge in a shadowy corner of the patio far from the rest of the party, wiggling his toes below the waterline as he peers at the mosaic on the bottom, a depiction out of Greek mythology, a laughing Dionysus standing in a shimmering golden chariot drawn by prancing leopards across a background of stars and swirling planets. Surrounding this chariot is a retinue of drunken satyrs, centaurs, and cherubs, all nude, dancing while sloshing fat jugs of wine. Several of the more menacing-looking satyrs brandish erections as fearsome as pikes, which they thrust before them like weapons or use to sodomize a group of human worshippers who have fallen to their knees in ecstatic veneration of the passing god.

Though this strikes Benji as an odd choice for pool decor, it certainly sets the mood for this party: After dinner, their host handed out little gray Quaaludes to Benji and the other boys and cheerily announced that they were, "To loosen us all up and make everyone feel groovy."

Benji managed to spit his into the pool without anyone noticing. He was already lit enough from the Valium he swallowed earlier, followed by several shots of spiced rum from their host's liquor cabinet. As he gazes up at the stars erupting from the twilit sky in droplets of sizzling white lava, he relishes the luxury of being left alone for once. Unlike at most of the recent parties he's attended, he's even managed to keep his swim trunks on so far this evening.

Too bad he's the only one.

Peals of laughter emanate from the hot tub several yards behind him where the others have congregated. He keeps his back turned to them. In the many years of unemployment, since the network canceled *Sandcastles*, he's learned not to watch the goings-on in the hot tubs at these sorts of parties. However, it often proves difficult to avert his eyes from the spectacle of a sagging, hairy-backed film producer or studio executive getting an underwater hand-job from a fresh-faced wannabe young enough to be his grandson. It's only human nature to rubberneck at the sight of something that grotesque, and yet he knows if he were to watch, he would need to keep a straight face and avoid betraying even a glimmer of the revulsion he feels. He'd have to maintain the illusion that this was a normal occurrence, perfectly natural, nothing to see here, folks. After all, it's never wise to appear uptight or judgmental, especially around powerful men who can handsomely reward you for being their good time.

Who can make you a star—or return you to being one.

Besides, it's not as if Benji *wants* to look. He doesn't need to see himself reflected back in the hopeful, determined expression on some grasping young wannabe's face. Been there, done that, too many times to count. He knows too well that those few precious moments in control are the most powerful you'll ever feel in this business, or at least until it's over and the big shot *has* shot and already forgotten your name.

Still, though he's managed so far not to watch, it's proven much harder not to listen.

"Oh, that's so dirty ..."

"I swear, he had no gag reflex at all ..."

"Have another drink and you won't even feel it ..."

"I bet he taught you how to do that thing with your tongue ..."

"Benji ...? Where's Benji?"

This is from that paunchy horror novelist who's been pawing at him all evening. The one their host brought in to help punch up the script for his new project. Although Benji supposes the man could be a useful ally to have, he sounds woozy and vaguely distraught at Benji's absence, which is reason enough to avoid turning around to acknowledge him.

Not that Benji will be missed for long.

"Screw him!" one of the other boys cackles, overzealous in his inebriation. Although Benji still likes to imagine himself and the other actors here as "boys," they're all technically men now. In this business, 18 is the new 40, and at 21, he feels unaccountably ancient. "I wanna sit in your lap, Daddy," this one coos shamelessly, and with a splash and giggle, the burble of conversation soon gives way to squelches and groans.

Benji stares into the silken darkness above the Pacific, trying hard to shut out all the unpleasant images swirling in his brain. He sips his drink and kicks at the water. He's grateful for this time alone. He's been off his game since he arrived here for the weekend. The vibe just doesn't feel right at this place. Something about Palazzo di Bacco sharpens the uglier edges of things that normally blur in L.A.'s permissive haze. He knows he should be in the hot tub with the others, making the most of this chance to ingratiate himself with that French financier with connections across the industry. But the thought of doing so makes his skin crawl. Not that he is above such friendly persuasions. He's been hustling for work his entire adult career. Nothing he will do this weekend will be any different from the kinds of things he's done at a dozen other parties just like this one. He's mostly gotten used to it by now, used to the unsavory ways it makes him feel, used to not caring. But here, tonight, it gnaws at him. Everything about this evening gnaws at him, though he isn't sure why.

Maybe it's Asa Barnstable.

The thought arrives from his subconscious with the urgency of a telegram. He takes another sip of his drink and tries to figure out what it means. The role he has his eyes on in their host's new picture is a modest but important one: Asa Barnstable is the naive American seminarian who gives up everything, including his life, to battle an ancient evil threatening to overrun the people of a small Greek island. Benji has never wanted another role as badly as he wants this one. It isn't just that securing a part in a major studio film would resurrect his moribund career, even if it is just a cheesy ripoff of *The Exorcist*. No, Asa is special. From the first pages of the script, the character resonated with some unspoken longing inside of him, a bass note struck on the tuning fork of his psyche. Although there are many qualities about Asa that he admires and wishes he could emulate in his own life, above all it's the selfless purity of Asa's faith that moved him most deeply. Asa meets his death peacefully, even joyfully, content in the knowledge that he is the chosen vessel of the Lord's grace. Such a sacrifice seems incomprehensible to Benji, even sacred. He has never loved or believed in anything strongly enough to surrender so completely to it. He doubts he ever could, although he wishes to experience what that feels like, to borrow just a glimmer of Asa's inner light.

It might be the closest he ever gets to shining his own light.

This is the true gift of acting, or at least Benji hopes so. He wants to believe that inhabiting a character nobler than himself can unlock little stores of his own humanity otherwise unavailable to him, little discoveries of qualities within himself that he might never reach in another way. When he thinks about it like that, acting becomes an almost spiritual endeavor, as close as he will ever get to touching the face of God, submitting to something bigger than himself, something that, even in its own humble way, can still be profoundly meaningful. When he thinks about it like that, he supposes he just wants to be worthy of Asa Barnstable, worthy of playing this righteous young man who gives up his life in sacrifice to the divine.

And yet, the irony of this entire weekend is that Benji knows nothing he will do at Palazzo di Bacco to "audition" for the role will make him remotely worthy of Asa.

Not one fucking thing.

He drains what remains of his drink and debates whether to grab another. More rum might help to blur the edges a little bit faster. At these parties, there's a tipping point when the booze and drugs flip a switch in his brain, either in the pool or hot tub or laid out across the cool sheets of somebody's waterbed. Like Paul Newman in *Cat on a Hot Tin Roof,* he feels that mechanical click inside himself, and his body gives way, ebbing into the liquid pleasure of the moment as freeing as pissing underwater. That's when the lights go out inside him, and something darker and hungrier emerges to feed, some creature like a vampire at twilight or a werewolf at the rising moon.

Maybe he needs that creature now. Maybe it will keep him safe tonight. Maybe it will hold Palazzo di Bacco at bay.

Or maybe it will just eat him alive.

A shiver runs down Benji's spine as a shadow falls upon him from behind. He glances over his shoulder to find a stranger looming above him, blocking his view of the hot tub and the other partiers. Benji tries to scramble to his feet, but the whole world heaves onto its side, and he nearly topples headlong into the pool.

The young man grabs him by the forearm and eases him gently to his knees.

"Please relax," the stranger says calmly and soothingly. "There is no need to get up."

"Who ... Who are you?"

"I tend the pool."

The stranger holds a hand for Benji to shake, but Benji's too dizzy to take it. Instead, he bends forward on his hands and knees to inhale deep breaths to clear his head. At least the patio stops spinning, although the moans emanating from the hot tub have become so vehement they sound more like cries of agony than ecstasy.

"I'm, uh, sorry about them," he stammers, his face flushing hotly as he sits back on his knees. The others obviously have yet to notice they have company.

"They merely enjoy themselves," the pool boy says dismissively, flashing a brief smile toward the hot tub. Benji supposes if he "works" for their host, he's witnessed this sort of thing before, probably even joined in a few times.

The pool boy leans over to shift Benji's empty highball glass aside and then squats beside him at the water's edge. "You, on the other hand, do not seem to be enjoying yourself at all," he says, grinning, his teeth glinting white then blue-gray in the refracted light of the rippling water.

His thick, dark brows arch in curiosity above fathomless black eyes that keenly search Benji's.

Although the pool boy's intensity is unsettling, Benji is too drunk to be intimidated, and he holds the pool boy's gaze long enough to take stock of him: Dressed all in black, the young man is likely around twenty-five. He has an East Coast look about him, vaguely ethnic, perhaps Italian or Greek, with pale skin and long, black hair pulled into a tight ponytail.

Jim Morrison meets Pacino.

Still, while he's certainly not unattractive—indeed, his looks are downright arresting—Benji detects an off-kilter aspect to his features, something vaguely unbalanced, asymmetrical: eyes inched too far apart, a mouth a fraction too wide, a longish chin too narrow and sharp. In fact, with his dark attire and piercing gaze, he reminds Benji more of a predator who's skulked into their midst than the kind of sun-kissed Malibu rent boy he'd expect their host to keep on the payroll. He flashes on what happened to Sharon Tate after the Manson Family paid her a surprise nocturnal visit and tries to shake off the images that follow by drawing this pool boy out.

"What's your name?" he asks.

"You may call me El," the pool boy says coolly.

"El? That's an odd name. What's it short for?"

"Why must it be short for anything?"

Since Benji has no answer for this, he shrugs, although not before noticing that there's something odd about El's voice. It has a satiny resonance to it that reminds him of a violin playing a low, sustained note. El's speech patterns are peculiar, too, stilted and formal, like he learned to speak English reading textbooks or really old novels. Perhaps he's Eurotrash. While it's a bit sexy, it also makes Benji uneasy. Worse, El's rapacious grin has not wavered, while his eyes remain fixed on Benji. Devouring him, Benji thinks. And the pool boy doesn't seem to blink or even breathe. Benji feels overwhelmed by this attention, yet it's also undeniably exciting, even arousing, and as he finds himself longing to succumb to the allure of El's seductive composure, he realizes that he's already leaning in, breathing slower, heavier.

"Where have you been hiding all evening?" he asks, swallowing the tremor in his own voice.

"I would not call it hiding."

"What would you call it then?"

"Observing."

"Why not join in instead of just observe?" Benji jerks his head at the hot tub. "Maybe you'll get discovered, become a star."

El chuckles lightly at this, as if amused by a child's innocent question. "Though I do perform from time to time, I do not consider myself an actor."

"What do you consider yourself then?"

"A student of human behavior, perhaps. Or, more accurately, of human desire."

"You mean like sex?"

Although El hesitates long enough to arch a prudish eyebrow, Benji suspects the question has secretly delighted him. "While I do not relegate my interests to that area of human experience alone, sexuality is certainly a fascinating aspect of desire, would you not agree?"

"I would." Benji smirks, half to himself, certain now that El is coming on to him. He must have spotted Benji from inside the house and pegged him for an easy mark. Perhaps he wants to fuck a former child star. He wouldn't be the first. Perhaps Benji will even let him. "Tell me more," Benji says, and drags his fingertips across the taut skin of his chest.

"Imagine what an observer would make of this evening," El replies, his tone suddenly expansive, academic. "Such a rich tableau of human desire on display, no?" He gestures grandly at the hot tub. The sounds of the orgy have receded to a background drone. "Your colleagues over there seek fulfillment of their baser hungers for physical pleasure and sexual gratification. But there are other, subtler desires at play, too. Desires for money, success, fame. The hunger for affirmation and the approval of authority. The need to feel powerful and strong, or perhaps to surrender, to be meek, compliant. A longing for beauty and the elusive blush of youth, or simply the desire to feel desired. To be seen and chosen. To be consumed." He pauses meaningfully before adding, "Perhaps there is even a desire for love."

Benji can't help but laugh at this. "Trust me, nobody here is looking for love."

"That may be," El agrees, his lips curling in a cryptic smile. "But while all of these desires are readily identifiable among your busy friends over there, what remains enigmatic to me are the desires of the lonely figure sulking by the pool."

"I wasn't sulking," Benji replies sulkily. "And they aren't my friends."

"Of course." El tongues the corner of his mouth. "But you still have not answered my question."

Benji hesitates, uncertain where this is going. "I thought what I desired was obvious: a part in your boss's new picture."

"Ah, I see. You wish to become a star like the others. Famous. Adored."

At this Benji mouth pulls into an involuntary frown. His legs have gone numb from kneeling too long, and so he takes his time shifting position, mulling over his response while he swings his feet around and dips them back into the languid pool. To be honest, he's surprised by how stung he feels that El apparently hasn't recognized him at all.

So much for wanting to fuck a former child star.

"Maybe you didn't know this about me," Benji mutters bitterly, "But I *am* a star." He leans back on his hands and gazes up into the burning night. "Or at least I was. For three whole seasons I played the irascible kid brother, Tony Pavone, on *Sandcastles*." He pauses, hoping for a reaction that doesn't come. "I made the cover of *TV Guide* once .... No?" He sighs. "It doesn't matter now. Former child stars are a dime a dozen in this town. Since we got cancelled, I haven't had so much as a call-back for a soap commercial. Casting directors either can't see me as anyone other than the mouthy brat I played on that show, or they assume I won't accept scale anymore. Not that I was ever a big enough star to warrant paying more. We didn't even film enough episodes for syndication, so there's no residuals to speak of, no money coming in. So, not only am I an unemployed star, I'm also a broke one. A star so hard up for work I've been reduced to hustling for jobs at hot tub parties." He laughs at the ridiculousness of his plight before turning to meet El's appraising gaze. "Being a star doesn't mean a fucking thing to me. In fact, it's meant worse than nothing, because it's kept me from doing the only thing I want to do, which is act."

Benji feels his face flush, shocked by how much he's revealed to this pool boy. It must be the rum and Valium talking, or maybe the way the hard edges of things keep showing themselves so clearly tonight. He longs for his comforting blurs and clicks to return, although he has to admit it feels liberating to have gotten all this off his chest for once.

Not that El appears the least bit fazed by his candor. If anything, it seems as if he knew just exactly what Benji was going to say all along. "Do you suppose you will win the role you so desire this weekend?" he asks. "That coveted opportunity to act again?"

The question feels like a sharp kick in the gut, or maybe just a bucket of cold water thrown in Benji's face. He remembers what his agent warned him right before she dropped him:

They never cast the whores, Benji.

"No," he answers as the dream of playing Asa Barnstable dissolves into the mist above the Pacific. "No, I don't suppose I will." There won't be any big break this weekend. No comeback. No coveted film career. As with all the other parties like this he's attended, he'll be lucky to leave Palazzo di Bacco with "gas money" in his pocket and without another case of the clap.

"Then why come here?" El asks, with what sounds like genuine curiosity. "Why do this?"

Benji shrugs and kicks at the water. "There's nothing else. I've got nothing else." He flashes El a bitter smile, but doesn't add what he's really thinking:

I'm here to feel wanted.

"Desire can be a thing with chains." El looks Benji dead in the eyes. "Perhaps yours has dragged you under."

"Sure …" Benji turns to peer into the pool, too ashamed to hold El's gaze any longer. "Why not." He wonders how what he'd imagined was a harmless flirtation could have led so swiftly to the edge of this cold and hopeless abyss. Maybe if he weren't still so drunk he could muster the dignity to climb into his car and leave this place before he humiliates himself any further.

But who is he kidding?

"Fuck it," he says and slides his swim trunks off his hips, launching them with a sharp kick into the far end of the pool where they float like debris from a shipwreck. "Let's skinny dip."

Finally naked, he stumbles to his feet and leaps into the water.

Despite the lateness of the hour, the pool is warm, even hot. The water feels strange upon his skin, silky and viscous, like taking a bath in amniotic fluid. He lets himself sink to the bottom and then kicks off, breaching the surface with a loud gasp, before inhaling a lungful of sandalwood and pine from the candles still ablaze all around him.

El has climbed to his feet and stands at the edge of the pool watching over Benji with that same wolfish grin as before. Benji winks teasingly at him and then arcs his spine, floating onto his back with his arms and legs splayed wide in an invitation. As his head lolls back in the surging water, he stares up into the night sky, thick and coursing with blackness.

The stars have all gone out.

El is speaking now, though his words are muffled by the water sloshing around Benji's ears. Benji thinks he hears him say something about "sacrifice" and "failure." Something about "purpose" and "veneration" and "the gift of being chosen." Something about "chains" and "liberation" and "the blessing of surrendering to the desires of God." It occurs to Benji that maybe El belongs to some sort of cult, like the Moonies, or one of those dirty communes up in Humboldt County were the Summer of Love curdled into a cesspool of drugs, false prophets, and ritual child abuse. Maybe he's a wannabe Jim Jones here to lure Benji to some far-off jungle compound to demand he perform deranged acts of devotion.

Not that it matters. Not that Benji cares.

He'll still fuck El tonight.

As the moments tick by, Benji realizes El has stopped talking. He lifts his head from the water to find that his companion has wandered off beyond the lights of the patio. Instead, he notices there's an odd new song playing on the radio. Unlike the thumping disco anthems he's been listening to all evening, this music has a meandering cadence like the accompaniment to a procession, with lilting flutes and bells, and indistinct voices floating above the steady thunk of what could be a tribal drum or perhaps the pulse of his own heart throbbing in his ears. It's like no pop song he's ever heard before, and as he lays his head back in the water to wait for El's return, he closes his eyes and lets himself drift on this music's primal, hypnotic strains …

"Come, drink this."

Benji blinks, startled by the sharpness of El's command and aware that he must have dozed off. His eyelids feel heavier now, his limbs sluggish as he paddles back to the edge of the pool, where El squats, holding out a shallow ceramic bowl with handles on each side. It takes Benji a moment to recognize the object. During the requisite tour of the house when he first arrived, their host spent several minutes bragging about this particular treasure, which he described as "the pride of my antiquities collection." A "kylix." He explained that it was an ancient kind of chalice, used by the Greeks for serving wine during "their deviant rites and ceremonies." Glazed in glossy black, the outer surface of the bowl is adorned with red-figured depictions of various Satyrs and men engaged in acts of debauchery reminiscent of the scene at the bottom of the pool.

Benji laughs, mumbling something to El about their host murdering them both if he were to catch them using his priceless antiquity as a Solo cup. But that doesn't stop him from grabbing the bowl from El's outstretched hands. He lifts it eagerly to his lips, his body aching with an unquenched desire for blurs and clicks, so much so, he doesn't even bother to ask what's in the bowl or why El's serving it to him this way.

If the sexy pool boy wants to be the next Jim Jones, let him.

Instead of poisoned Kool-Aid, however, the kylix contains a kind of sickly-sweet wine, viscid and cloying and smelling vaguely of honey. Some part of Benji's brain suggests it's probably mead, although he's too busy guzzling every drop to give it much thought. When he finally swallows the last of it, he notices that painted at the bottom of the bowl is the figure of a single, penetrating eyeball staring him in the face.

He hands the precious artifact back to El, wipes the stickiness from his mouth, and exclaims in his most seductive voice, "Get out of those clothes and come join me."

But El merely shakes his head as he rises to his feet, backing slowly away from the pool. "I will see you on the other side," he says before he turns and strides across the patio cradling the bowl reverentially between both hands.

Benji watches him disappear into the house, feeling lightheaded and vaguely dismissed, although he assumes El's just gone to replace the bowl on its glass-encased pedestal in the living room. That's wise. God forbid they should get caught with it out here. Benji doesn't want any trouble this weekend. He certainly doesn't need to make enemies of powerful men like their host, although he doubts the famous director would even remember his name if he were to slip away from Palazzo di Bacco before morning. The boys here are all so interchangeable:

Kenny and Mikey and Jamey and Davey. Warm, nubile bodies good for a night's pleasure, a weekend's play. A currency of skin and sex. Cogs in a flesh machine older than Hollywood itself.

Still, it's better than the alternative. Benji would rather be here than home alone. He'd rather feel desired than nothing to no one, a forgotten credit on a cancelled TV show.

And so he floats onto his back to await El's return.

He hopes El will take him right here where the others can watch. He's never actually done it in the pool before. Foreplay yes, but for the main event he's always been led to a bed, a sofa, a countertop. He finally feels that soft mechanical click as his body eases into the liquid pleasure of his drunkenness. The strange music seems to grow louder on the radio, and he closes his eyes and floats, wondering what exactly El gave him to drink. Was it really mead, or perhaps some kind of exotic liqueur or imported sherry? He'll have to ask, although whatever it was, he can still taste its warmth on his lips as its blurring potency seeps through his limbs, giving him an urgent, throbbing erection.

When will El get back? he wonders, while in the distance, the roar of what sounds like a mountain lion echoes across the hillside.

The music stops.

Benji jerks open his eyes at the sudden silence, but instead of the placid Malibu sky, he peers stunned into an impossible celestial tableau wheeling above him.

Palazzo di Bacco is gone, along with the patio, the hot tub, the others.

In their place, an inky expanse of firmament arches high overhead, bursting with a million silver-bladed stars. Sulfurous clouds veil a moon as pink and fat as a boar fed for slaughter. A livid Mars hangs so low to the earth, Benji thinks he might reach up and pluck it from the heavens. Shrouded in golden mists, Venus hovers beside it, while slender rings encircle Saturn's delicate saffron orb, and Jovian satellites speed in obedient orbits around the many-banded tyrant of worlds. Surrounding these planets are galaxies and nebulae too numerous to count, swimming and swirling like stellar amoebae in an iridescent sea of sky. And yet daylight also shines here, banishing the night around him with the brightness of a solstice noontime.

The Sun itself is a whirling disk of white.

Under its hard, prismatic glare Benji sees that he now treads water at the center of a perfectly round and viridescent pool. This pool is surrounded by a ring of ruined columns strangled in heaving vines of ivy and fruiting grape. The columns are ancient, their pediments pitted and crusted with lichen, their crumbling scrolls draped with fronds of swaying moss. Beyond them stretches a flourishing garden that perfumes the sultry breeze with rosemary and honeysuckle, lavender and oleander. Spiky succulents intermingle with jeweled blossoms of scarlet poppy, indigo anemone, buttery nasturtium. In the distance, limpid pools of vibrant turquoise ripple tremulously beneath swaying boughs of fig and olive, while further beyond a colony of towering cypresses clings to a gently sloping hillside that meanders down to a ribbon of quartz sand and the shimmering expanse of a cerulean sea that is decidedly *not* the Pacific.

The heightened color and light in this place hurt Benji's eyes. Dazed and uncertain, it takes him several moments to realize he seems to cast no shadows here. This pool itself feels only half-real to him. A dreamscape. A shaman's vision. A hallucination of tainted mead.

Or perhaps *he* is the hallucination, insubstantial, a projection across time and space.

But before he can ponder the meaning of any of this, a low moan behind him calls his attention. He splashes around to find that behind him the ring of columns opens onto a rise of steps that lead to a sloped marble altar overlooking the pool. Splayed face down upon this altar is a nude figure, his arms and ankles lashed by leather straps to massive bronze chains anchored to the stone. His skin is golden, his buttocks clenched as he writhes against his bonds. The ropey muscles of his arms and legs flex in weary desperation. Yet these efforts prove futile—the straps are drawn too tight—and soon he gives up, collapsing against the hard surface and falling still.

Although the young man's long hair spills over his face in curls of corn-spun silk, Benji immediately recognizes himself, like watching a projection of his own performance on-screen.

But, no—this figure *is* him.

Once more, Benji tries to pull against the straps binding him to this icy slab. It's no use, of course: The leather is too supple, too strong, although the heavy chains of bronze creak and rattle like the bars of a dungeon cell. He is drenched from head to toe in sweat—or pool water?—his body spent, exhausted. He lays his forehead against the marble to rest, but above the lingering scents of chlorine, sandalwood, and pine he detects a faint coppery tang.

It smells like …

He jerks his head back, strains and wriggles against his bonds until he sees that below him, in the very shadow his chest and arms now cast, the altar is stained the deep russet of dried blood.

The music resumes with a swell.

Benji hears the approach of footsteps behind him, a procession, bells and cymbals and many voices singing in a language not his own, though one he somehow understands.

"Hail, Eleutherios, glorious liberator!" they sing. "Lord of the lustful. Patron of the wanton. Seeker of the flesh."

Benji cranes his neck and can just make out a line of nude figures dancing and singing. Some are playing instruments, while others carry fat jugs of sloshing wine as they proceed in single file around the edge of the pool and gather along either side of the steps at the base of the altar. Although these figures are all clearly male, none are human, sporting tails and antlers, wings and horns and even hooves.

When the last member of this motley procession has reached his place beside the altar steps, the music dies. An ecstatic hush falls over the crowd until another roar pierces the silence.

"Behold, Eleutherios!" a chorus of joyful voices sing. "Deliverer of desire!"

And that's when Benji sees it, rising like the kraken from the center of the pool.

The beast towers more than fifteen feet tall. Although its features vaguely resemble El's, they are courser, fearsome. Its lustrous black hair is wild and unkempt beneath a fat crown of vines adorned with flowers and golden thorns. Its fathomless black eyes are no longer eyes at all, but gaping voids filled with galaxies of rushing stars. Its horns are made of gleaming gold, as is its angrily swollen cock, thrust outward, the length of Benji's leg and the girth of his thigh, tapering to an eviscerating point.

Green water sluices from the beast's massive body as it lumbers from the pool toward the altar. Benji squeezes his eyes shut tight, too frightened to look upon such staggering glory any longer, although he can still smell the fetor of the beast's breath, its arousal, its vileness. He hears the crowd gasp, followed by the clack of mighty hooves upon the marble steps behind him.

But before it is there, before it can claim him, a brilliance shines within Benji, revealing to him why he was chosen for this sacrifice, this veneration. A gift of selfless devotion, of love, his whole body and soul subsumed in the role of his lifetime. All he ever wanted and all he ever was, surrendered for all eternity in this holy place.

His chains are broken. He will touch the face of a god.

"Please, Eleutherios," Benji cries. "Please!"

Then the beast is upon him.

Only Castles Burning

A week after I told Fergus I'd proposed to Abby, he woke me at two in the morning with a text that they'd lit up a hellhole in Mecklenburg, and we had to go see it before it burned out.

I sat in bed as I read the message and immediately shivered. Dad had splurged on a big chunk of our winter gas ration during Christmas break to keep Aunt Sarah warm, and now he turned the heat down so low the house was like a refrigerator at night. I could see my breath as I squinted bleary-eyed through the frost that glazed the window beside my bed and imagined how warm and toasty the fires of hell would feel right about then. Outside, the moon hung in the clear night sky like a forty-watt bulb somebody had flicked on in the basement to keep the city's pipes from freezing, but it wasn't working. Ice encrusted the cars and houses along my street, while the university buildings on the far hill glinted like blocks of quartz in the silver glow from the snow and moon and stars.

I scanned the message again and slammed the phone on the bedside table. I was pissed that Fergus had woken me for a goddamned hellhole after a week of dead silence. But he was always getting worked up over crap like that, crap he couldn't do a thing about. It was just like him to get twitchy because the gas company had lit a match to a sinkhole in some farmer's lower forty. Here was a kid who trolled the eco blogs like most guys hunt for porn. When he was twelve, he even wrote a letter—an actual, honest-to-God *letter*, with a stamp and envelope and everything—just because the Starkist people started putting dolphin meat back into the tuna fish. My attitude was, well, what's left out there for them to put in it? But he went off and wrote his letter, and six months later, he got back a coupon for five bucks off his next can of tuna.

That was pretty cool because at least it meant a real person had opened his letter and read it, but he got so worked up about it that he had an asthma attack and was out of school for two days.

I snuggled back under the covers, shoved my face beneath the pillow, and tried to conjure up the dream I'd been having about Abby doing that thing she does with her tongue, but my phone buzzed again.

It was Fergus texting he'd meet me out front in fifteen minutes.

I almost texted back, *Piss off.* Almost. But since I could count on a single hand the number of times we'd actually hung out alone together in the months since graduation, I climbed out of bed, dressed, and went outside to sit inside my truck and shiver my ass off until he showed up.

He was there in the fifteen minutes he'd promised. Fergus was never late, especially when he was on a mission. He drove his mom's ancient Prius with the

Cornell bumper sticker on one side and, on the other, the one that screamed IF YOU'RE NOT OUTRAGED, YOU'RE NOT PAYING ATTENTION. I sat there idling for a minute because I figured if we were heading all the way out to some cow pasture in Mecklenburg, he might see it'd be smarter to take a 4X4. But I should have known better. Fergus hated my truck because of the shitty mileage and wouldn't ride in it to save his grandma from certain death.

"Screw this," I said after he'd flashed his high beams at me about a dozen times. I didn't want him to start honking and wake my folks, so I pulled the key from the ignition and got out. There was never any point in trying to win a war of wills with Fergus. So be it if we got stuck out in the middle of nowhere. Maybe then he'd realize it sometimes made more sense to be practical than righteous.

I slid into the passenger seat, and he nodded at me, his face shining beet red in the overhead light, maybe from the cold, his irritation, or too much caffeine.

When my seatbelt was on, he threw the car into reverse and backed us into the road.

"I baked you cookies," he said.

He reached into his lap and tossed me a Ziploc bag filled with waxy brown lumps the approximate size and shape of gluten-free, organic poodle turds. I knew they would taste about as good as they looked, but with Fergus, it was only ever the thought that counted.

"I guess this means you're speaking to me again," I said and stuffed the bag into my coat pocket, but he didn't respond.

It would be unkind to say that Fergus was a dirty hippie, but damn if he didn't go out of his way to look like one. Although he couldn't help being scrawny any more than he could help his asthma or the acne that burst like fireworks across his face, he could've at least paid enough attention in the mirror to do something about his hair, which was a red rag-mop that dangled across his shoulders in greasy snarls, as if he'd used it to swab the insides of a deep fryer. He wore his gramp's green and black checked hunting jacket, red Cornell sweatpants, and a rainbow-colored Tibetan yak's wool scarf with little pompoms on the ends his mom had knitted for him when he was, like, ten. But even though he'd probably forgotten to shower for a couple of days, his breath, at least, still smelled as sweet as licorice from the Mukhwas seeds he chewed instead of gargling with corporate mouthwash.

"They lit up the well," he said. "Poof. About eight o'clock last night."

He turned to me as if expecting a reaction.

I shrugged. "Happy Fourth of July?"

"Carl said they had to do a controlled ignition because the gas from the leak was building up too fast, and they were afraid it would cause a major blowout. Like the one that killed all those workers in North Dakota."

"What happened to the rig?"

He forced a laugh.

"What do you think happened? It got sucked into the hole—that's what happened."

"Was anyone hurt?"

"Dunno. Probably not or it would have made the news. Not that anyone cares."

He swerved the car onto Route 79 and gunned it straight up the hill. The front tires spun on the frozen pavement, and we nearly skidded into a car parked alongside the curb, but then he eased up on the accelerator, and the worn-out treads managed to chew their way back to traction.

"Carl said it's a big one ... Maybe even an acre or two."

"Who's Carl?"

"Just a guy I know from school who runs this website that tracks hellholes. He hacked into a video stream they broadcast to their corporate headquarters and saw when they lit it up. Said the fireball shot about 200 feet in the air and vaporized all the snow around the perimeter."

"Jesus," I said, still wondering about this Carl dude and why Fergus hadn't mentioned him before. It was weird to think there was this whole other part of his life now, filled with strangers from the university I would probably never know. He must have felt the same way about the guys from work and me, and I know I'd blindsided him with the news about Abby. But still, I couldn't help wondering about all the other Carls in his life. What did they have to talk about anyway? The energy crisis, climate change, and the start of the next ice age, blah, blah, blah.

Not that he and I had so much to talk about anymore.

"It's still on fire," he said, like even he couldn't quite believe it. "Carl said the gas pocket's a deep one. Might burn for days. Even a week."

"Jesus Christ, you mean it'll be there in the morning? Why the hell did you wake me up? Take me home. I need to get to church in a few hours with Abby and her folks."

His back stiffened at the mention of her name.

"Now she has you going to church, too?"

"It's no big deal. It's just for her folks."

"Whatever ..."

The thing was, ever since the day Fergus popped his first boner, he'd acted as if he didn't have the hots for me, and I'd played along like I didn't know it was all an act. It was easier between us that way, although sleepovers and locker rooms had been a little dicey sometimes, what with all the pretending not to look or notice being looked at.

But that was all right with me because Fergus was just being Fergus. We'd been best friends for pretty much as long as I could remember, although nobody could understand why. Not even our families. Pops was an electrician at the BorgWarner plant, and Ma ran the kitchen at the high school, while Fergus's mom was an ecology professor at Cornell, and his dad had been a big-time environmental activist with Greenpeace until he got shot protesting some pipeline down in Pennsylvania.

I guess his dad dying like that, so young, I mean, was maybe why Fergus was always such a serious kid. Even in middle school, he would only ever talk to me about important stuff, big stuff, like life and death, nature and the universe, the future of the planet, and what we were doing to it. When we got older, he talked a lot about Thoreau and Marx, because he understood that shit and wanted me to get into it with him. It was like he thought I could be just as smart as he was, like I wasn't just another one of the boneheads in our class who never formed a complete sentence that didn't include the words beer, baked, or pussy.

And that was pretty cool.

Thing is, most guys don't *talk* to each other. Not really. Not about stuff that matters. But with Fergus, I could talk about anything. And if I sometimes said something ignorant or didn't understand what he meant or where he was coming from, he never made me feel stupid. We'd just talk it through until it finally clicked.

So yeah, it was fine by me if he stole a glance at my ass now and then, or brushed up against me in the shower after gym. Whatever. It was cool. I never judged him, and it's not like it changed anything between us.

At least, not until I proposed to Abby.

After we'd been silent a while, he said, as if reading my mind, "Do me a favor and forget about Abby for once.

Things have gotten weird lately, and I just want to hang out tonight like we used to, okay?"

I didn't reply. I knew "weird" was Fergus-speak for shit neither of us wanted to get into, like how I never even asked him to come with me to pick out the ring and what that meant about our friendship. It didn't matter that he'd known since eleventh grade I planned to marry her someday. He thought it was all happening too soon, though as far as he was concerned, forever was probably too soon.

I understood where he was coming from. I hadn't even asked him yet to be my best man because I felt it, too: Change is the suckiest part of the natural order of things.

So instead, we let it lie. Fergus flicked on some earthy folk music on the stereo, and I just stared out the window. The streetlights petered out as we reached the top of the hill and crossed the city limits. We passed the sign for Rachel Carson Way on the left, where they'd put up the gasworks on the site of the old Eco Village. Fergus once explained how a bunch of educated hippies had built their own private commune there until the gas company offered them ten million bucks for the land where they grew their organic hemp and tomatoes. They sold out and moved to Mexico.

As we drove by the facility, the gigantic spherical holding tanks glowed in the moonlight like a half-dozen enormous snowballs poised to roll down the hill and crush the city. Beyond, the countryside unfurled in every direction, with fallow fields, naked trees, and darkened house trailers tucked snugly beneath the same shimmering blanket of snow.

When Fergus finally couldn't stand the silence between us anymore, he started in about the hellhole. I figured he'd had all evening to get himself worked up about it, and I was right. He began by lecturing me on all the damage mass implosion fracking was doing to the land. He said there was barely enough gas left in the Marcellus and Utica shale to make extraction possible anymore, but the drilling companies and the government kept at it, using whatever ridiculous means they could to get at the dregs.

"They're basically setting off bombs underground, man … That's what mass implosion really means, you know?"

I just nodded because it wouldn't do any good to point out how many times we'd already had this conversation.

Then he started complaining about the dozens of other hellholes across Pennsylvania, Oklahoma, Texas, and the Dakotas. He said it was only a matter of time before New York was covered with the same gigantic pockmarks. Only a matter of time before we had the earthquakes, the poisoned water and air. But nobody around here seemed to care.

"They just want to heat their fucking houses," he said with disgust. "Everybody moans about how bad the winters are now, but nobody wants to admit climate change made it that way. Like, everyone thinks it's too late to worry about it anymore. I can't even get a decent student protest organized on campus because nobody can be bothered to fit it into their social calendars."

I just kept nodding. I'd heard it all before, and it was just as depressing as ever, especially since, lately, it'd begun to sound like he thought some of it was maybe my fault, too. Because of Abby, or because I'd taken the job Dad got me at the plant instead of going to community college. Because I was settling for my life the way it was instead of how Fergus thought it could be.

I tuned out his rant as best I could until the guitar-strumming hippie on the stereo warbling about the icebergs on the Amazon or whatever plucked my last nerve, and I asked him what the hell we were listening to.

He flashed me a smile that lit up his face like dawn breaking. "You like it?" he said. "It's a playlist Carl made for me."

"Oh," I said because now he was sharing music with this Carl dude, too.

Then I turned back to the stars.

Once, when we were fourteen or so, I caught Fergus jerking off to a pair of my boxers. I'd crashed at his place this one weekend when some friends of my folks came to visit. It must have been five or six in the morning, and I was asleep on his bedroom floor in his gramp's musty old army sleeping bag when I heard something that woke me up. I didn't know what it was at first, but when I opened my eyes, I saw Fergus on his futon silhouetted against the first rays of the dawn, breathing heavily and going at it fiercely with my underwear draped over his face.

I'd never seen another dude beat off before, let alone use my sweaty boxers to get himself going. But it felt like it wouldn't be cool to interrupt him, so I watched, all transfixed like I was one of those scientists in a nature show, hidden in the bushes and filming the never-before-seen mating ritual of some exotic, endangered species. It didn't even feel weird, just private and off-limits. I was even grateful that he trusted our friendship enough to risk doing it with me in the room.

Anyway, it was a good ten minutes after he'd finished and fallen to sleep that I rolled onto my back to relieve my own morning wood. Still, I couldn't keep Fergus out of my mind, and afterward, I couldn't fall asleep again, so I just lay there until he woke up, wondering what it was he'd done to me in his fantasy and what I'd done to him.

I never said a word about it to him, though, and I never took my boxers back. But that was cool. I even left another pair under his pillow when I crashed there a couple of months later.

It was well after two in the morning by the time we got to where we were going. Fergus took a sharp left onto some back road and gestured toward a faintly glowing patch of sky above the hill in the distance. It'd gotten so cold outside the air was dusted with tiny flecks of ice that floated like dandelion seeds in the beam of the headlights. Although I'd turned the heater all the way up, our breath had begun to crystallize inside the windshield.

As we approached the hilltop, the road veered sharply to the left and ended a few hundred feet below at the entrance to the rig site. The gate was thrown wide open, and we drove straight through. Though the incline was steep, the gas company always kept their access roads plowed better than the county highways, and the front tires didn't even spin as we made our way up the hillside.

Ahead, a small patch of stub evergreens was lit from behind by a dazzling orange glow. Above the trees, whirls of steam and snow danced in the light. Pellets of sleet began to pepper the windshield out of a clear night sky, and I realized that the heat from the hellhole was making its own weather. The ice crystals on the inside of the windshield began to defrost. Glimpses of dead grass and brown earth poked through thawed patches in the snowpack, and we even splashed through a fat puddle of melted water. Then the road veered sharply around the evergreens and ended all at once in a steaming gravel parking lot that had disappeared into a lake of fiery light.

And there it was.

It was easily the most out-of-control thing I'd ever seen in my life. It was like God Himself had hauled off and punched a hole in the ground. Huge slabs of turf had collapsed into the center of an enormous, blazing crater at least a couple of football fields across. Hundreds of small flames jetted up from tiny vents scattered throughout the rubble at the base of the pit, spewing columns of smoke and steam and waves of heat into the sky. At the center lay the remains of the rig—thick shafts of twisted, melting steel.

I looked around, but we were the only ones there. I'd half expected to see a gang of rig workers passing a toke, some high school kids taking selfies along the edge, or at least the poor bastard farmer who'd leased the field that had just become the biggest bonfire in the Finger Lakes. But not even a potbellied crew from the Mecklenburg volunteer fire corps was on hand to keep the situation under control, and in spite of myself, I felt disappointed. It was sad to think something this awful had become routine. It was like we were witnesses to a murder scene that nobody had even bothered to report to the cops.

Fergus turned off the ignition, and we climbed out and walked around to the front of the car. As soon as I opened the door, it felt like I was stepping into a wood stove, but it was so wonderful after that frigid night ride that I shucked out of my coat and gloves and dropped them onto the hood of the car so I could soak up as much of the heat as possible.

"Can you believe this shit?" I said or rather shouted because the roar of the thing was like a rocket taking off. "My whole block could fit practically inside it."

I leaned back against the hood and watched as crazy patterns of steam and smoke swirled up from the flames, creating a vacuum that sucked in what looked like these impossibly fat snowflakes from over the tops of the evergreens that edged the perimeter. These were carried aloft on the riled eddies of superheated air, whirling and flitting before the pit drew them down into its burning core.

It took me a minute to realize that these weren't snowflakes at all. They were moths, dozens and dozens of them, defrosted from their winter cocoons and lured to their deaths by all that heat and light.

Fergus leaned in close beside me and said, "It's like staring into the face of the devil."

"Forget that hellfire shit in the Bible," I said, reaching out to warm my hands as if the thing in front of us was nothing but a cozy campfire. "If the devil exists, he's cold as ice, man. Cold as ice."

I took a couple of steps toward the pit. The heat felt like heaven against my hands and face, and I closed my eyes and let it soak into me like a shot of 100-proof tequila. It was so intoxicating that I almost didn't notice when Fergus trudged past me and stepped up to the rim.

"What the hell are you doing?" I shouted after him. "Don't get so close."

"Carl wants some video to post." He pulled out his phone from the pocket of his sweatpants and began to shoot. "I'll be fine."

"Is that why we're out here?" I demanded, suddenly amazed by how much I could hate this jagoff Carl dude without having even met him.

"It's not the only reason."

Fergus panned the phone's camera across the broad expanse of the pit, then squatted down and leaned in way too close to the edge to focus on the wreckage at its core.

"Why didn't Carl come out here himself to take his own damn video?"

"Because he doesn't have a car."

I started to say, "But *you do*," when it dawned on me that it wasn't Carl he'd asked to come with him tonight.

Score one for me.

So, I kept my mouth shut while he shot the rest of his video, though I followed closely behind to make sure he didn't fall in as he edged the perimeter with the phone planted in front of his face. He was so careful to capture every detail of the scene, from the carnage of the rig to the death dives of the moths. As he filmed, Fergus narrated, rattling off random facts and figures on recent blowouts at other sites, estimates on the amount of greenhouse gases released into the atmosphere, projections on the volume of carcinogens dumped into the water table, what the harm to local wildlife would be, and so on.

At some point, my head began to swim with all the data he spewed out, and it occurred to me that Fergus knew more about this single subject—only one of the dozens of issues that kept him outraged daily—than I probably knew about pretty much everything in my entire life.

The thought made me feel small.

It wasn't until we went almost the entire way around the pit that Fergus finally stopped filming. All at once, he shoved the phone back into his pocket and stood there, poised a few feet from the edge.

"Sometimes I wish I were one of those moths," Fergus said as I came up beside him. His voice had gone raw and tired, and he stared into the hellhole. "I wish I could just flit around soaking up the heat, not knowing or caring about what was really going on."

"You mean like me?"

"No, not like you. At least you listen. You even try to understand."

I shrugged. It didn't feel like I was trying to do much of anything tonight except keep warm.

"What's to understand?" I asked. "Shit happens."

"But you're here, aren't you?" he sounded as if he wanted to prove to me I was wrong about myself. "Look around. That's more than I can say about anybody else."

"I wouldn't be here if you hadn't dragged my ass out of a warm bed."

He sighed. "This isn't about you, okay? It's about everyone. I'm just so sick of people. The whole human race. We turn everything to shit, even the ground beneath our feet, and nobody cares at all."

"Come on, man. Not *nobody*."

It wasn't like it was the human race's fault that Fergus had lived his entire life believing he could move the world if he just bashed his head against it hard enough. If it wasn't water pollution and climate change, it was the dolphins, the rain forests, or the goddamned African tsetse fly. There was always something that needed stopping or saving, somebody's consciousness that needed raising.

I squeezed his shoulder, "Not *everything's* turned to shit. We're still here, man. You and me. Nothing's gonna change that."

Whether or not I believed it was true, it was clearly the right thing to say. He flashed me this awkward little smile, like the kind the kid gives at the end of a Band-Aid commercial, and then he reached out and took my hand into his, squeezing it like he thought I might go fluttering off into the hellhole if he didn't hold me back.

I didn't pull my hand free. Maybe because we were all alone, or because he'd made me feel sorry for him by talking like that, or because I still felt guilty over how badly he took it when I broke the news about Abby and me.

Or maybe, if I'm honest, it was that his hand was warm and felt so good in mine.

But whatever the reason, we stood like that a long while, side by side, holding hands and gawping at the flames together, and I was thinking, *Well, if this is as weird as it ever gets between us, it's still pretty good,* when Fergus wheeled around, grabbed me by the back of the neck and kissed me, hard, sucking on my mouth for dear life like he was frantic to get at the air in my lungs, his boner jammed up against me and the warm, sweet flavor of the Mukhwas seeds on his breath filling my mouth.

I didn't pull away.

But the next thing I knew, he'd pushed himself off of me and was struggling to catch his breath, like he was about to pitch into an asthma attack or something. His face crumpled, and he drew his hand in front of his mouth and mumbled some half-assed apology I could barely even hear. He swiveled his hips to conceal the hard-on tenting his sweatpants and looked away from me as if afraid I would be angry. But all I could think was that I wished he hadn't stopped kissing me because when he did, he'd taken all the heat in my body with him.

"Oh shit." He backed away. "Why did I do that? I don't know why I did that. Why does everything turn to shit? Absolutely everything."

I didn't know what to say, so I didn't say anything. I straightened my hoodie over the front of my jeans to hide my own deflating erection and stumbled back toward the car, feeling as if I'd just been freeze-dried from the inside out.

A gnawing in my gut awakened the memory of the baggy of organic, gluten-free cookies Fergus had baked for me. I pulled it out of my pocket and popped one into my mouth, but no matter how hard I tried, I couldn't convince myself it tasted any good. I gobbled the rest, anyway, wishing they would somehow fill the emptiness inside me.

Fergus didn't follow me. Instead, he walked up to the edge of the hellhole as close as he could get and stood staring at the flurry of moths that kept flitting to their stupid deaths in the belly of flames.

By the time I reached the car, I was quaking all over from the cold. I wrapped myself in my parka and gloves and scrambled inside.

I watched Fergus through the windshield for a while. He was so close to the fire and smoke and steam, I began to worry about his asthma and wondered if Carl knew that he kept an emergency inhaler inside the glove compartment. A part of me hoped that he didn't.

When Fergus came back to the car, he'd turned beet red all over again. I couldn't tell if it was from the heat or his asthma or from something he was too embarrassed to face.

We didn't bother to look back at the hellhole as we drove off, as if ignoring that heartbreaking thing might make it go away, and though I wanted to reassure him that it would all be okay, that none of this mattered, that we were both going back to where we belonged, I didn't say a fucking word.

The Dancing Bears

June slumps behind the steering wheel, her face burning with irritation as she peers through the downpour at the empty shell of Jerome's dilapidated rental house. Things are not going according to plan. After a half-hour of waiting, Jerome is still nowhere to be seen. The rain hasn't let up one bit all afternoon, and although she hoped to scandalize Mama with the low-cut blouse she wore for her mission here, Mama merely scoffed when she saw her.

"Put on a sweater before you leave this house," Mama commanded, as June sucked in her breath to puff out her chest as far as it would go. "You'll catch your death in that getup, you ridiculous girl."

Then she laughed, the way she always laughs at her only daughter.

June deflates all over again thinking about it now. But it's no matter. Though she did what Mama told her to do and slipped into a sweater before sulking out the back door, as soon as she reached the car she tore it off and threw it defiantly into the back seat.

Today she will show Mama what she is truly made of.

Today she will change her fate forever.

Today she will win back Jerome.

She will, that is, if only he finally comes home.

She peers at his dumpy new rental house, deciding it's an improvement over the dorms. Set further back on its overgrown lot than the other homes in this rundown subdivision, the little ranch reminds her of a mangy white rabbit cowering behind the bushes and shedding its flaking paint like clumps of fur onto the un-mown grass. The windows are dark, the garage door left open, the garage itself empty save for a few scattered packing boxes, painting supplies, and a sofa propped against one wall.

In the distance beyond the house, two police helicopters circle an enormous paint can-shaped balloon floating in the rainswept sky above the shopping plaza behind the subdivision. Today is the 14th Annual Big Tony's Paint Oasis Extravaganza. June listened to Big Tony himself doing a radio promo for the event on the drive over:

"We've got coupons for free pints of paint and free painter's caps for the first thousand customers. Plus, we've got a Ferris wheel, cotton candy, and a tamed polar bear named Daphne that's gonna dance jigs for the kids!"

The balloon is the exact shade of feminine-hygiene-product pink as the Paint Oasis logo, and June wonders if Big Tony is at the other end of its tether, preaching the gospel of proper priming to his customers as they line up under their umbrellas for cotton candy and pictures with the dancing bear. The thought gives her a sinking feeling, as if she were missing out on some kind of bizarre spectacle by waiting around for Jerome like this.

He has to come home eventually, she reassures herself, and glances down at the sack of peaches on the passenger seat beside her. She toys with the idea of texting him again, but quickly rules this out. She texted him earlier to say that she was on her way, and he responded almost immediately that she absolutely should not come. She texted back that she wouldn't, but she was pretty sure he didn't believe her.

Now he's probably staying away on purpose.

For weeks he's refused to answer her texts, DMs, emails, phone calls, tweets, chat requests, and the letter she sent by registered mail. She was surprised that he bothered to answer her message today, even if it was only to tell her he didn't want to see her.

He claimed he was *2 busy* and would *B painting all day long.*

Pete sends his love.

Ha! As if that would keep her away.

She checks her make-up again in the rearview mirror, fingering a fleck of mascara from the corner of her eye. She pouts her narrow lips and daubs on more lip-gloss. Then she powders away the shine from her cleavage. Johanna calls the silk blouse she lent her "continental," because it hangs off her shoulders in a plunging V and clings to her breasts like a second skin. For the first time since junior high she's foregone a bra, and she is pleased that the sensation of her bare nipples brushing against the blouse's silky fabric feels provocative, even indecent. She decides she's successfully created an aura of moody sensuality about herself, just like the women in those awful French films Jerome used to force her to watch. She'll make him see that she isn't just another high school girl. She'll make him regret what he lost when he dumped her.

She leans back in the seat, drums her fingers on the steering wheel, and gazes up at the foolish pink balloon, wondering absently why anyone would go to the trouble of training a bear to dance jigs for the amusement of paint buyers. It seems like an awful lot to ask of a stupid animal, not to mention cruel and inhumane. She feels a stab of grief for the poor, caged creature, until she remembers the bedtime story Mama used to tell her when she was a little girl about a dancing bear who was tricked into a cage by an evil witch, and only managed to escape once she realized that cages are only cages until you break the lock. After Mama caught Daddy with his secretary, she broke the lock on their unhappy marriage. With her newfound freedom, she rewarded herself with new breast implants and true love, remarrying a rich and successful doctor, no less. Now she drives a Mercedes and lives in a house with five bathrooms, while Daddy and that tramp Beverly Manning have to make do with a Chevy and a two-bedroom condo.

Cages are only cages until you break the lock.

June intends to break the lock of her own cage with Jerome today. She will succeed using Mama's own secret weapon: unblinking certitude. Mama always gets her own way by never doubting that she will get it. This is the quality about her that has changed the most since the divorce, a life skill she's honed until she mastered it, nagging the minister into finally admitting Jesus was a Republican, browbeating salespeople into giving her the wholesale discount, and seducing her plastic surgeon into dumping his fiancé and marrying her instead. But whereas Mama only learned to break out of her cage after twelve long years trapped in a loveless marriage, surely June will do her one better. She won't accept her breakup with Jerome as the final answer to their chance for happiness. She will accomplish what even Mama couldn't with Daddy: She will force Jerome to love her again, no matter that he's decided to become gay all of a sudden.

Maybe then Mama will finally take her seriously.

She grabs her phone and is about to snap a selfie with the house in the background to prove to Johanna she came here, when it rings in her hand.

"Have you turned him back from the pink side yet?" Johanna says as soon as June answers.

"Shut up. He's not even home."

"Where is he then?"

"I don't know." June forces a laugh. "Avoiding me? Buying more paint?"

"What are you doing then?"

"Sitting in the driveway, waiting."

"Pathetic."

June holds her tongue as she wipes the fog from the windshield with the sleeve of Johanna's blouse.

"How do you even know he's not home?" Johanna asks. "Did you at least knock?"

"No. But it's obvious."

"And you don't know when he's coming back? It could take all day."

"No, it won't. He left the garage door wide open and there are boxes and drop cloths and empty paint cans all over the place. When he texted me—"

"He actually texted you?"

"Yes, of course," June says, proud that she's forced him to relinquish the silent treatment, even if only by blackmailing him with the threat of a visit. "Jerome said he was painting the living room. He just ran out for more paint or something. He'll be back soon."

She sounds so convincing, she almost believes herself.

"You better not get any paint on my blouse," Johanna says, and June can tell from the clatter of hangers in the background that she's rifling through her closet.

"Don't worry. I plan on taking it off as soon as possible."

Johanna sighs. "Seriously, June, I know I've said this to you about a thousand times already, but this is easily the craziest idea you've ever had. What if Pete shows up?"

"He works today."

"How do you even know that?"

"Because Jerome always tweets about being left alone on Saturdays."

"You're such a stalker!"

June chooses to ignore the remark. "Peter Ryan won't be back for hours yet," she says, using his full name like she always does, as if somehow that makes him less of a threat. "And by then it will be too late."

"Too late? Do you seriously think this insane plan can work?"

"I wouldn't be here if I didn't," June says and drifts into silence. As she already explained to Johanna, her secret weapon is the peaches. She did her research. She read an article that said you should always attract a boy's attention to your mouth if you want him to kiss you. These peaches are extra ripe. She selected them carefully. She imagines biting into one, how the juices will flow down her chin, how she will lean in to Jerome and lick her lips seductively, how the scent of the peaches on her lips will be so sweet and appealing he will have no other choice but to kiss her.

Jerome likes peaches. *A lot.*

She glances at the small, silver-framed picture of a smiling Jerome that dangles from a silver chain affixed to the car's rearview mirror. In the picture he wears only a red Speedo and the shiny bronze diving medal he won at an NCAA tournament. He is so very handsome with his wavy black hair and dark, defiant eyes. It makes her ache all over just to look at him. She especially likes the way the water glistens on his bare skin, the way he cocks his hips just to the left, how the still-wet bathing suit clings ever so subtly to the parts of his anatomy it barely conceals ...

"You'd better not get any peach juice on that blouse," Johanna says, dousing the tingle of warmth that's reached its way deep into June's core.

"I'll be careful," she says.

"You know this is never going to work, don't you?"

"I'll make it work."

Johanna makes a big show of sighing again. "Why won't you let this go? He likes dick. Don't you get that?"

"No, I don't," June says, trying not to raise her voice. "I told you before, he's not really gay. He's just confused and sexually frustrated. I held out on him too long. He doesn't know what he wants or what's best for him. Peter Ryan is just a shot in the dark."

"Are you even listening to yourself?" Johanna says, and June can tell from the sound of hangers slamming one against another that she's become angry again, like she did the first time they had this argument. And the second. And the third. "This is the stupidest crap I've ever heard in my life. Jerome is gay. *Period.* Why can't you accept that?"

"Because I love him."

"You don't love him, June," Johanna says, just as the sky bursts open like a severed artery. "This is only about getting your own way."

June lets Johanna's words fade into the pummeling din of the rain before she speaks. "Look, I don't expect you to understand this. I love Jerome. *I love him.* And I know deep down he still loves me. I just have to make him see it again."

Johanna shouts, so loudly her voice makes the phone's tiny speakers crackle, "But he's shacking up with a dude!"

"That's my whole point," June says, as calmly and rationally as she knows how to be. "If Jerome had slept with another girl, it would have been like he was cheating on me. So, he didn't do that. Instead, in his sweet, confused way, he picked Peter Ryan to cope with his sexual urges instead of one of those sorority sluts. Don't you see? He chose a gay boy to spare my feelings. Peter Ryan *proves* he still loves me."

"Oh my God. You've turned into your mother."

"Okay, I have to go now. Bye." June slams the phone onto the passenger seat.

She tells herself that Johanna is just trying to be a good friend but obviously lacks vision. Johanna feels she understands affairs of the heart more fully than June because she's dated three different boys and lost her virginity at sixteen. To her, love is something to be used and made worthless in the using, like the disgusting condoms that litter the woods outside the dorm where Jerome used to live.

June knows better. She fell for Jerome the first time she laid eyes on him at church and decided on their very first date together that he would be the one someday. Only, she waited too long to prove herself to him, and he grew tired of waiting. But it isn't too late. All she needs to do to win him back is to convince him that her devotion is unwavering. She will give him what he wants, what he needs. What all boys *need*. And then they can be happy together just like it was always meant to be.

She glances at the clock on the dashboard. She's been here forever and still no sign of Jerome. The rain drumming against the roof of the car can't drown out the pounding of her heartbeat, and it suddenly occurs to her how she must look sitting out here all alone, like the pitiful ex-girlfriend waiting to be let inside the gay boys' love nest to reclaim some left behind possession or to make a brave face at remaining "friends."

She decides this waiting around is pathetic and grabs the sack of peaches from the seat, opening the car door to the deluge and nearly tumbling to the ground in Mama's best heels as she scrambles out of the car. Police sirens wail in the distance as she scuttles into the garage with the paper bag over her head to keep her make-up from running down her cheeks. She calls out Jerome's name, but there is no response. The door leading inside has been propped open by a paint can, and as she climbs the few steps into the kitchen, it occurs to her that any criminal can waltz right into this house. She wonders at how reckless Jerome has become since letting Peter Ryan into his life but then stops abruptly as she crosses the threshold.

A swath of devastation greets her inside the house. The kitchen looks like a war zone. Cardboard boxes are strewn across the floor and torn to shreds. Broken dishes lay like shrapnel on the countertops. Shattered jars ooze innards of peanut butter, mayonnaise, and lurid sauces she can't begin to identify. Streams of beer flow across the linoleum floor from the trampled remnants of a six-pack. At the knees of the gaping Frigidaire, a carton of milk purges itself into a white pool.

Resting face down within that pool is Jerome's crushed cell phone.

A barrage of questions fires through June's mind: Has there been a fight? Did Jerome break up with Peter Ryan? Has the gay boy gone insane? Is Jerome lying injured somewhere, helpless and bleeding?

She hears a muffled voice coming from deeper within the house.

He needs me, she thinks and clutches the bag of peaches to her chest as she staggers through the ravaged kitchen toward the voice.

As she enters the hallway, the raw stench of urine and wet paint nearly overwhelms her. The green shag carpet is stained and damp, as if someone has relieved himself on the floor. Spots of blood are splattered along the baseboards like buckshot, and a smear of blood is spread into a grimace across the freshly painted white wall. From the open doorway ahead, June hears a low glugging sound, as if someone is downing a pint of liquor, and it's then that the muffled voice resolves itself into a familiar image in her brain:

Big Tony. A radio is on somewhere. Another commercial. That's all it is.

Only, as she rounds the doorway to the bathroom, another voice interjects. "That was Anthony "Big Tony" Cardillo whom police say was badly mauled earlier this afternoon when the trained bear he ..."

On the cool green tiles of the bathroom floor slouches an emaciated polar bear lapping lethargically from the toilet bowl. The bear is almost entirely pink, save for runnels of white that show through from where the rain has washed away the feminine-hygiene-product pink dye that colors its fur. The creature drags its broad pink head up from the toilet bowl to glare at her in the doorway. Black nostrils flaring in rage, the animal pants in labored exhalations. With agonizing slowness, it turns its body to face her and then slams the floor with its massive pink paws, causing the entire house to tremble.

The creature lurches forward, its head lowered, its teeth bared and gnashing.

June feels her knees begin to buckle. She staggers backwards just as the bear attempts to rear up onto its hind legs. But the ceiling is too low for it to stand erect, and it pitches forward, its right forepaw slashing at her.

June screams, but before she's eviscerated, strong hands grasp her by the shoulders and yank her into the pantry closet behind her, slamming the door shut with a muffled thud.

"June?" Jerome whispers into her ear, before the crackling impact of the bear's head against the door silences them both.

In case you were wondering, this is the bedtime story about that dancing bear Mama used to tell June when she was still a little girl:

Once upon a time, a bear and a fox struck a strange bargain with a witch for the elusive prize of becoming human. The terms of this agreement were simple: In exchange for granting their wish, the witch required that the fox and bear dance for her amusement for forty days and nights while locked in a gilded cage inside her castle, with only the cockroaches and grubs she provided them to eat. She warned that if they failed in any way to meet the terms of this agreement (or perished from exhaustion), she would fashion from their respective pelts a beautiful stole and a comfortable hearth rug.

If, however, they managed to persevere, at the stroke of midnight on the forty-first day, their fur would melt into smooth skin, and they would become as human as human could be.

The fox, who desired human fingers to make it easier for him to steal, quickly tired of dancing and did not care at all for the grubs and cockroaches he was given to eat.

Since he thought himself too clever to abide by the rules of the agreement, he snuck news of his predicament to his beleaguered wife and bid her to smuggle him nibbles of cheese and sweets through the bars of his cage while the witch dozed.

But alas, the witch was a very light sleeper, and upon awakening to discover this treachery (Mama occasionally suggested it might have been the bear who woke her up with a well-timed cough), she became so angry that she immediately killed both the fox and his poor wife, turning them into a stole and matching muffler.

The bear, however, was a far more sensible creature whose motives were pure of heart: She'd fallen in love with a handsome young hunter, who told her that he couldn't possibly marry her until she became human. (Not that this had ever stopped him from "tasting her honey," as Mama liked to say, although it'd taken June many years to figure out exactly what she meant by that.) The bear did not think herself too clever to follow the rules. She understood that no great reward is ever earned without greater sacrifice, and besides, she knew that dancing for forty days on a diet of only grubs and cockroaches would do wonders for her figure.

So, she danced and danced and persevered, and forty days later was granted her wish.

(It was only *after* the divorce that Mama changed the ending of this tale entirely, with the bear breaking the lock on the cage and devouring the witch—who had *never* intended to grant her wish to become human—and then, soon thereafter, devouring the handsome young hunter too, once she found him in bed with another bear.)

Anyway.

*

In the darkness of the pantry, June ponders her situation with measured optimism. Although they've been trapped inside this closet together for at least ten minutes now, Jerome hasn't spoken another word to her since her name. She wishes she could see his face and read his expression. She hopes his eyes are smiling at her, offering her silent strength, reassuring her that he will protect her no matter what fate has in store for them.

But since she can see nothing in the darkness, she decides to simply assume the best.

She hears Jerome shift against the wall and feels herself yearn for him to brush up against her. But although the pantry is barely large enough to hold them both, he's somehow managed to avoid touching her completely. She tries to recall how his body used to feel sitting next to her in the movie theater or bending over her to peck her cheek at the end of a date. She always longed for him to sweep her into his arms on those occasions, to feel the warmth of his skin pressed against hers, to know the taste of his plump, sweet lips. But somehow, he always sensed—even when she hadn't known it herself—that she wasn't quite ready to go that far, and so he held himself back, a perfect gentleman time after time.

She can almost punch him in the nose for his gallantry now.

It occurs to her that she should probably be more concerned about their predicament, but strangely she feels no unease at all. The bear seems to have fallen asleep on the other side of the door. They are safe in here together for the time being, and at least they are finally alone. It isn't exactly how she planned things, but still, this is the nearest she's been to Jerome in ages. If she squints at their situation just so, it's even romantic, the kind of endearing story to laughingly tell their grandchildren someday. *Remember, dear, that time we were trapped in the closet by the polar bear. You were so brave.*

June smiles to herself. She doesn't care how long it might be before someone comes to rescue them. The future is theirs now. They have all the time in the world to get there.

"It's nice in here," she whispers. But when no response is forthcoming, she repeats herself more forcefully, "I said, it's nice in here, don't you think?"

Jerome demands, "Where's your phone?"

"Uh, I forgot it in the car."

"Dammit," he curses, shifting in the dark. "Pete should have been back by now."

The sound of Peter Ryan's name feels like a cold slap. It's almost as if Jerome is trying to sour the mood.

"I thought he worked on Saturdays," she grumbles bitterly, but he doesn't reply. The thought that Peter Ryan might show up and ruin everything makes her sick to her stomach. It's so unfair. She deserves this time alone with Jerome, but he only seems to have other things on his mind. She senses his anxiety charging the air between them. She wishes he would try to relax and enjoy the darkness with her, but she can tell that he's too busy plotting their escape to pay any attention to that.

She hears the rustle of his hair as he gingerly presses his ear to the door.

"It hasn't budged for a while," he says. "I think it's asleep. It's in pretty rough shape. There was blood all over it, and I saw what looked like a bullet wound in its haunches. I think it would have smashed through the door by now if it could."

"I brought you peaches," she says. She holds out the bag to him, but he shoves it away with such force that she drops it, dumping the contents all over the closet.

Peaches bounce off the door and onto the shelves beside her, knocking over canned goods and echoing loudly in the confined space.

The bear stirs on the other side of the door.

Jerome curses her under his breath.

June presses herself back against the pantry shelves, stepping onto one of the peaches as she does so. The warm juice of squished fruit oozes into the crevices of Mama's shoe. For a terrifying instant the door creaks ominously as the animal leans its full weight against it. But then the bear seems to clamber to its feet and wanders off. A moment later she hears a soft groan followed by a thud, as the beast settles itself somewhere on the far side of the wall at Jerome's back.

It takes several more minutes before either of them dares to speak again.

"What the hell are you doing here?" Jerome finally demands, his voice restrained but steeped in anger.

"I just wanted to talk things through, to tell you I was sorry."

"Sorry for what? Stalking me?"

"No, no. For making you wait ... I mean, I wanted to explain what I realized about us."

"There is no *us*, June."

"That's not true."

"Yes, it is true. I'm with Pete now. Don't you understand that?"

"I understand a lot. I understand better than you think I do."

Jerome falls silent for a moment, and despite the darkness, June senses that he is watching her, appraising her for signs of self-doubt to exploit. It's the kind of thing Mama would do, and she thinks she has prepared herself for it, until he speaks.

"Did your mother put you up to this?"

She shouts, "No!" And then remembers where she is and lowers her voice. "No. Of course not. She doesn't know about any of this. Can you imagine what she'd say if she knew about you and—and *him*?"

She can almost hear Mama's voice: *What did you do to turn that boy gay? Only my daughter could ruin such a fine young man.*

"Why would you even think that?" she continues, but when Jerome doesn't respond, she realizes she's holding her breath, waiting for his answer.

"You do understand she already knows about me, right?" he finally says, so softly it takes her brain several beats to insert the necessary bits of meaning into the various words she only half comprehended.

"What?"

"Your mother. She knows I'm gay. She's always known."

"That's crazy. Of course, she doesn't know."

"Oh, come on, June, think about it. Do you really believe she'd let you date a college junior if she thought for a moment there was any chance of me getting you pregnant?"

"It's because she trusts *me*," June says.

"Your mother? When has she ever trusted you with anything in your life?"

The answer to this question is painfully obvious. June knows better than anyone what Mama thinks of her, how she talks about her in the company of others—family, friends, even Jerome—as if she is shoddy goods they might actually be foolish enough to buy.

"No, June," Jerome continues. "She trusted *me*. As long as you were busy holding my hand at the movies, you weren't out getting pregnant by some pushy high school kid."

June falls silent. It seems like the prudent thing to do while she works through the many layers of unpleasantness in Jerome's words. Of course, she knows Mama much better than he does, but just because what he said didn't occur to her first doesn't mean she can fault his logic. It's probably true. Mama believes Jerome is gay. It explains so many things.

But that doesn't mean Mama's right.

Mama doesn't always get to be right.

"I don't care what she thinks," she lies. "Let her think what she wants. This is about you and me. What we are, what we have. June and Jerome. Jerome and June. Even our names are perfect together. I love you and you love me, and you're just too confused to know it right now. But you'll see. I'll make you see."

She reaches out in the darkness and grabs for where she hopes she will find his penis but squeezes his elbow instead.

He slaps her hand away before she can make another attempt. "Don't you get it?" he snarls. "You were my cover, that's all. A sweet little church-going virgin to get my parents off my back and to keep them paying my tuition. But then Pete came along and changed everything. I changed. I realized I could stand up to them, stand on my own. I didn't need to hide anymore to get their approval, or the church's, or anyone's." He takes a deep breath, and when he speaks again, all the bitterness in his voice has melted away. "Look, June, I know how unfair this has been to you. I was cruel and selfish and weak. You deserve better. You deserve a guy who wants you, who'll love you for real. Not some coward like me using you to hide from himself. I'm sorry for that. I'm so, so sorry. But I need you to understand that this is over now. *We're over.* Please, Junie. It's time to move on."

June won't hear him, refuses to listen to a single confused word he says. She's too busy fumbling with the zipper of her skirt to pay his silliness any mind. She's already slipped off Mama's shoes and is sliding out of her skirt when he speaks again.

"June, are you okay? Please, say something."

But she has nothing to say. It's too late for words, too late to reason. So instead, she throws herself at him. She grabs for his head and hurls her arms around his neck, knocking him into a shelf of dry goods as she clamps her legs around his thigh. Jerome yelps and tries to slip free, but she shifts her weight against him and pulls him toward her, her fingers clawing at the back of his neck as she tries to kiss him once, twice, but only succeeds in biting his chin. With one hand still clenched to the base of his skull, she drives the other to where his belt buckle presses against her waist. But before she can manage to unclasp it, Jerome regains his balance and pushes her away.

"Are you trying to rape me?" He laughs. "Can this get any more ridiculous?"

June feels her body go rigid. She lets her arms fall away and slides to the floor, where she crawls into the corner beside a pile of old newspapers and begins to quietly sob.

Jerome stands panting over her for several moments before he speaks again.

"I don't know what that was all about," he says, his voice stern and steady. "But I'm going to forget it happened. I suggest you do the same." And then, as if the fact that she's just humiliated herself for him has had no more impact on him than a joke told in poor taste, he begins to rattle off his plans for their escape.

Though June doesn't listen, she does stop sobbing. Why bother with tears? Mama was right about her all along. She *is* ridiculous. Even Jerome says so. Sobbing only proves the point. And to think she came here believing she was breaking the lock on her cage, when in reality she's only been dancing to Mama's tune this whole time. Her blood runs as cold as the rain pattering against the roof outside. She starts to shiver, though she's too mortified to reach for her skirt on the pantry floor. Instead, she huddles against the newspapers, her knees drawn to her chest as she slowly rocks back and forth while Jerome drones on about his stupid escape plan.

"You go ahead without me," she interrupts. "I'll wait here."

"But—"

"I don't want you to look at me right now. Just go... *Please.*"

"Okay," he says warily, but instead of making a move to leave, he leans against the pantry door and lets out a long sigh. "I—"

"Go!" she snaps. "Before it wakes up or Peter Ryan walks in and gets hurt. Go, before you say another word."

"Alright, alright. But are you going to be okay?"

"Now you care?" She chokes back a laugh, but when he starts to answer her, she cuts him off again. "I am a grown woman." She pulls herself to her feet. "I will take care of myself." And then, as if to demonstrate her resolve, she stretches the pins and needles from her limbs and squats down to feel among the sticky remnants of the trampled peaches for her skirt.

"Alright," Jerome says, and she can sense him turn to leave. "I won't be gone long. I'll come back with the cops as soon as I can. Just close the door behind me and stay put until help arrives."

"I will." She takes a deep breath, noticing for the first time that he hasn't bathed recently. He stinks of sweat and turpentine, and she is glad to have him leave. Only when he is gone will she be able to breathe again.

Jerome cracks open the door, flooding the pantry with light.

June squints against the rush of illumination and gropes blindly for the doorknob. As she does so, her hand brushes against his. He yanks it away awkwardly, but she takes hold of the knob with dignity and forces herself to watch as he slips out into the hallway.

She doesn't shut the door behind him.

Instead, she listens for the soft squelch of his sneakers on the kitchen linoleum until she hears their rapid patter as he bolts across the concrete out of the garage.

Only then, when she is sure he's made it safely out of the house, does she throw the door open wide and step fully into the daylight.

Her eyes ache as they adjust to the brightness. She pauses to listen to the voice of the radio newscaster as he reports that the manhunt—bear hunt—has moved two miles to the north based on a possible sighting near a church parking lot.

As the shining world comes into focus, June turns to see Big Tony's enormous pink polar bear spread across the living room floor down the hall from her. The creature lays unconscious and inert, a gigantic and oddly serene spectacle in its woolly, pink repose. Although the rain still beats against the roof, sunlight from a break in the clouds streams through the living room window, setting the creature strangely aglow.

June walks slowly down the hallway, her skirt still clutched in her hand, her bare footfalls muffled by the carpet as she approaches the beast. Now that she takes a closer look, it's hard to muster much fear of this bear, which has been badly treated and seems gravely ill. Its back is bowed and twisted from years of living with shackles inside cages that were too small for its comfort. Its matted pink coat hangs loosely from its bones. Its ribs show through furless patches on its chest, and a ripely bleeding wound gapes at its haunches.

June feels an unforeseen welter of emotion toward this pathetic creature who, like herself, has finally broken the lock on its own cage, though at a terrible cost. She thinks of Mama, Johanna, and Jerome, and at last seeing herself through her own eyes instead of theirs, she steps up to her fellow dancing bear, kneels before its feebly respiring form, and with as much quiet care as she can muster, reels back her fist and punches it squarely in the head.

What We Leave Behind Us

A ghost resurrected from the altar of your remembrances, Loretta stands before you shucking mussels in a haze of practical ritual. A galvanized metal washtub perspires on the kitchen counter beneath her, its belly full of ice and mollusks steaming with cold. As if inured to the passage of time, she has remained the stubbornly plump, Italian matron of your boyhood. Her arms are still as doughy as unbaked loaves of bread, her bare shoulders still spotted with the same angry-red heat blisters that burst each May and pulse until late September. She still twists her hair into the pious white bun she's had pinned to the base of her skull since you were an altar boy, while the same golden crucifix you once gave her for Christmas dangles like a showy carapace of grievance covering her heart.

She hasn't felt your eyes upon her yet. A hot, comfortless breeze stirs behind you, and the screen door moans as the gust passes over your shoulders into the kitchen. She raises her face to greet the stirred air, and the thought occurs to you that this is the pose in which you've so often pictured her during the past two years: alone, sweating out the rites of her distaff atonement in silence; cooking for an empty table, cleaning up an empty house. The pleasure you've taken in the daydream of this lonely internment seems cruel now, and you long to feel something finer than this for her, something tender and affirming. You picture the suckling of cancer within her breast and wince at the pang of guilt that follows. Strangely, the sharpness of the sensation pleases you. It's been so long since you've let yourself feel anything at all about her that it's almost reassuring to realize nothing but love could still feel this dreadful.

As if she can hear your thoughts, Loretta jerks her head around, and your eyes meet. For a moment she stares at you as if she doesn't know you. Her confusion is not unwarranted. You've lost weight, grown a full beard. You're a man now, or at least somewhere along the constantly diminishing road to manhood.

Yet, recognition quickly dawns across her face. Along with what? A glimmer of resignation? You search her dead eyes for some deeper sign that she understands why you've returned home, yet there's nothing else hidden within her gaze, not even astonishment.

She doesn't even have the courtesy to flinch.

"Tony?" she asks, and the wary tone of her voice unnerves you in that same exposed way Dad's always did when you were fourteen and doing unmentionable things behind locked bathroom doors.

"Hi, Grandma."

"Well …" is all she says.

A beat of silence follows, then she waves you inside with a sigh that speaks eloquently enough.

You take a seat at the same chrome and cream Formica table that's hunkered down in this kitchen since before you were born.

She offers to make a pot of black coffee.

"It's too hot, but thanks."

She nods, and then gestures to the washtub. "Carmine's—your grandpa's dinner," she says. "On Fridays he likes my cioppino."

You remember.

She brushes past you, pushes a plate of stale biscotti in front of you, resumes her work. The chipped green dish of Stella D'oro gives you flashbacks to the set of Yogi Bear jelly jar glasses she once filled with milk for you at this very table. She doesn't seem to notice that you don't take any cookies, rapt as she is in her sacrament of domestic butchery.

You've been privy to this mussel shucking ceremony countless times before, but you can't help becoming absorbed by a grim fascination with her progress. She still possesses the terrible grace of a well-oiled killing machine. Her muscular breaths flex metrically as she works. Her wrist pivots piston-smooth as she manipulates the piss-colored handle of a flathead screwdriver, attacking the mussel in her grip with sharp jabs of precise brutality. She jimmies apart the elbow of the creature's shell with a swift twist and gouges into its inner ligature, shearing free the central mass of slippery tissue from its bone-colored fix on the inner casing. In an instant, it's over. With a plop, she dumps the mussel's inner self into a cast iron pot crouched in the double-sink and deposits the vacated shell into your old blue sand pail resting beside her feet.

As she picks up the next creature, the muscles in your back clench, as if you were witnessing some drunk in a bar fight about to take a knife to the throat.

"Carmine digs 'em out up to Sylvan Beach," she says, too abruptly. "He knows a good spot near the state park. They're good fried with linguine, too, but I don't like to waste the fresh ones like that."

"I remember," you say, mostly to remind yourself that you're not a stranger here.

"That's good." She turns to give you the once over. "I see you took off a few pounds. You ain't looking healthy at all." She underlines her disapproval with a few clucks of her tongue.

"I was too fat."

"Yeah? Well." She'll have none of this modern obsession for leanness. For a certain generation of Italian matron, robust corpulence is the surest sign of well-being. Food is life, after all. That's why so much effort gets put into it.

"Dad says I look good." You don't mean to sound defensive, but you'd really like to tell her she should worry less about your weight and more about her own. You could never understand how someone who worked so hard could remain so heavy. But then, obesity and dowdiness are next to godliness in this house. The Lord don't make time for those who make time for vanity. That's how she'd scold all the beautiful women on T.V. when you were a boy. Those *puttanas* on her afternoon shows.

At the time you hadn't realized just how beautiful your own mother had been before she ditched Dad and dumped you at Loretta's feet like a bundle of dirty laundry needing to be sorted out. It was Loretta who boiled the stains out of your jockey shorts, darned your socks, let down the hems of your pant legs. You can still hear the hiss of her old Singer machine that used to slither under the covers like the serpents in the Bible stories she'd make you read aloud to her before bed. Those snakes kept you tossing and turning all night long. You've dreamed of them your whole life since, even slipping between your hairy, grown toes, and up the insides of your hairy, grown thighs, each with the beady yellow eyes of sin, and a forked tongue whispering rumors of your own guilt, like the Devil himself come to offer you the apple of knowing and shame as he did for Adam and Eve.

"Bad one," she mutters, and drops an un-shucked mussel into the blue bucket by her feet. "Shell's open. It'll be dead awhile. They'll make you sick if you ain't careful."

You nod, but she doesn't notice. She's avoiding your eyes.

"It's a blessing to your dad for you to come home for a visit like this," she says, rolling her shoulders to stretch. "We're all gettin' so old."

"It hasn't been that long."

"I didn't say it was …" She trails off in that pointed way of hers that always said a thousand times more than her words ever could.

She doesn't leave you long to stew over the innuendo though, because then she's asking about your job, your students, your commute in the big city, what the other teachers are like. All the safe, polite, meaningless questions you'd expected. She could be an acquaintance at a party, your barber, someone next to you on an airplane filling the void with idle chatter, and at first, you find yourself responding with all the safe, polite, expected answers. This is the dance, each of you taking turns leading the other harmlessly away from questions about your personal life, where you're sleeping nights, with whom.

But then you blurt, "I met someone," because you haven't come here to play safe anymore.

"Yes," she says, and in the high, heady light of the sun-drenched kitchen, you think you see her shoulders tremble, ever so slightly. "I do keep tabs on you, you know." She inhales deeply, as if about to say something more. But she doesn't.

Your palms begin to sweat, and you wipe them against your jeans. You close your eyes and listen to the lustful buzzing of the August cicadas outside. There is a kind of luxuriance in avoidance, a kind of solace in holding your words at the brink. You savor it for as long as you can, even as your whole world feels poised on the edge of this single, unspoken truth.

"Did dad tell you his name?"

She says nothing at first but tilts her face into the sunlight bearing down through the window above her. From where you sit, the light seems to cast a kind of aura around her head, as if she were radioactive, burning off an inner fire emanating from deep within her body.

She stares into that fierce light a long while before speaking softly, softly. "Ah, yep ... He mentioned it." Then nothing more. Nothing at all.

You grab one of the Stella D'oro from the plate to force something into your mouth before your hurt can come tumbling out. Nothing can become a reality in this house until she speaks its name aloud. Not even love.

Yet, silence is the only dialogue she's ever known.

The cookie is dry and hard and scratches your gums making them sore. You want to ask her for milk, a lullaby, a kiss on the cheek, a story of what you were like as a little boy. But you don't because you can't abide your own neediness.

Neither could she.

So instead, you ask her if she knows how to atone for a hard heart. Even to your own ears this sounds like an accusation.

Outside, the clouds pass over the sun, and the world between you dims. She turns to look at you again as if

WHAT WE LEAVE BEHIND US

she doesn't know you, as if you are a complete stranger, some brazen punk who's walked in off the street and kicked his muddy boots onto the top of her clean kitchen table. Bereft of the sunlight to ease the brutality of years, you notice the wide-set shadows beneath her eyes, the penetrating lines of care engraved into her face.

She is ashen, ghostly.

"I-I don't know, Tony," she finally says, stung into humility. "I guess you pray to be forgiven."

"But what if there's nobody there to listen to your prayers?"

"There's always somebody."

"But what if—?"

"Well, I guess you'd be on your own then."

You can see that it pains her to say this, and you're ashamed that you're glad of it.

"That's what I've thought, too," you say, and reach behind into your back pocket to retrieve your wallet. "Sometimes you have to answer your own prayers."

You remove the photograph of you and Ted on your first anniversary, arms entwined, kissing, and step towards her, the picture dangling from your fingers like a poisoned apple.

"What's this?" she says, reaching for it.

"My fiancé."

Something flashes across her eyes. Something like panic. She drops her hand without taking the photo.

"Look at it," you insist.

"No." Her voice is granite. The weight of it pins you down. "I'm ... I'm all covered in guts and gore, and I still gotta do the eels yet." She turns back to the sink and grips the edge of the counter as if wanting to make it bleed.

At first you are too stunned to move or speak. But then she commands you to fetch the cutting board from the top of the refrigerator, and all at once you are ten years old again. With the picture still in hand, you trip over the leg of your chair, clumsy in your adult-sized feet, and stumble into the old Frigidaire as it wheezes like a terminal relation in the back corner of the kitchen. You snatch the cutting board and pass it wordlessly to her.

"Thanks," she mutters, slamming it onto the counter. She yanks open a drawer beneath it and retrieves a frightening cleaver lying in wait amongst a menagerie of kitchen detritus. In the other well of the double sink you notice a school of small eels swarming in a brine of yellow water.

"Carmine and his eels," she mutters under her breath and snorts.

"I should go," you say, suddenly exhausted as you stagger back to your chair.

But she doesn't respond, and you watch her numbly as she reaches into the water and snatches an inky black eel, grasping its tiny head between her thumb and forefinger. The thing squirms as she pins it against the cutting board and brings the cleaver down with the implacability of a guillotine, severing its head from the remainder of its writhing body. Its carcass roils, a thin stream of blood spurting off the board and onto the countertop.

It's a brutal sight, and you gasp.

"A nasty business, ain't it?" she says with unexpected sympathy. "I hate cooking with these damn eels, but Ma always said they held all the flavor in the stew."

"I remember," you whisper, a billow of disgust rising within you as she grasps the next eel.

"Ma always said you gotta do it quick and firm to make it painless. You can't hold back or the knife won't go all the way through, and then you'll just make the thing suffer." She slams the cleaver down again, and your entire body flinches. "Oh, how I used to holler when I was a little girl and she'd make me fix the eels for the stew. I wouldn't wanna do it. It'd make me so upset. I didn't wanna hurt 'em, you know? But she'd grab ahold of my wrist as hard as she could and make me swing down that knife like it was a hammer. *'Rapido e costante!'* she'd say, *'Rapido e costante!'* Quick and firm to make it painless. Anything else is cruel ... That's how I learned to make her cioppino."

"I really should go." But you can't pull your eyes off the pair of eels on the cutting board, their final dribs of life flowing out in a watery slough onto the countertop.

"She'd say, there ain't no use in feeling bad about it cause we all gotta eat to live."

"It's getting late—"

"It's the way of the Lord, she'd say. It's how he made the world to work."

"Dad has errands for me to run—"

"Ma was right. No matter what, we gotta eat to live. We gotta get by somehow." She says this with the gravity of a deeper intent. She turns to face you, placing the cleaver on the countertop and wiping her hands on the waist of her dress before stepping towards you. "We all gotta get by somehow," she repeats, "Even if it means being hard sometimes." She says this as if comforting a child and takes hold of the photograph from between your fingers. "Let's put this away now," she says and gently tucks it into your shirt pocket.

It's such a brazen and direct act that you nearly succumb to its finality.

But you don't.

"Is this how you get by?" you say and slam your palm against your pocket. "Turning a blind eye to what you don't want to see?" The words drop like acid from your tongue, but she only gives you a bemused smile, as though the answer to your question were so obvious it never even occurred to her that you'd ask.

"I get by with the help of the Lord."

"The Lord?"

"Yes, Tony, our Savior." She says this with such certainty, such clarity of thought and simple, honest faith it almost seems like a put on. So much so, you're half unsure whether she's the one who's spoken the words or some other, cynical voice reading from a script inside your own imagination. "Don't you believe that the Lord is your Savior?" she continues. "Ain't that what I always taught you?"

"What?"

"The Lord. You believe in the Lord, Tony. I know you ain't given up on Him yet."

She smiles at you, and it's a disturbing, hopeful expression.

"I don't know what I believe," you say feebly.

"That's not true."

Her eyes are on you like tender prods.

"I don't believe in anything, okay? Let's drop it. I need to go. Let me go." You try to take a step backwards, but your feet are sewn to the floor. You don't have the will to pull them free.

"Tell me you believe in the Lord," she insists, and you imagine that her voice has grown sonorous and dire, like the roar of an onrushing tide. Your eyes lock onto her steady gaze. Outside, the clouds have drifted past, and the high summer light streams in through the window. It crests over her shoulders in a golden shower, pure and blinding.

"What I believe in is the truth."

"But there ain't no difference," she says, and reaches out to seize your wrist. Only then do you realize you would have collapsed years ago were it not for her strength holding you upright. "If truth's what you believe in, then I think it's time for some hard truth."

The light shines all around you now, flooding through the window. Its warmth lands on your cheek, and yet it isn't the sunlight at all that you feel, but her hand, caressing your face with such tenderness, the calluses gone from her fingers, the hardness from decades of toil erased. Her touch feels only supple against your skin, as mild as a loving word; her eyes filled only with acceptance, as deep and heartfelt as you have ever known in all your other dreams of this moment.

"The truth is I waited too long," you admit, softly, broken again. "I'm so sorry I waited until it was too late."

She lets go of your face, your wrist, and passes back to the counter.

You must grip the edge of the table to keep from falling. You want to bolt for the door to escape this despair, but you can't slip free of the torrent of grief sluicing out from this empty release. The warmth of her touch has ebbed away too quickly. You will not be so easily saved.

"You'll come for dinner tonight?" she asks casually, as if nothing had just occurred between you. Then she picks up the cleaver from where she left it on the counter and retrieves the next eel. "I know Carmine will wanna see you … Ask about school."

The thought occurs to you that this is just what you would have her say, and yet you feel overwhelmed not by the gesture of phantom redemption, but by the keenness with which your memories and regrets have conspired to take on a seductive life all their own.

"I'm sorry I wasn't here at the end," you whisper.

"You'll like that, won't you?" she asks, as if she hasn't heard you at all. "I'll bake some fresh bread to go with the cioppino. Maybe make a tomato salad—"

"So sorry ..."

"We'll fatten you up, yet," she says emphatically, and plucks another eel from the sink. "You'll see." She dispatches it as effortlessly as if nothing had ever interrupted the flow of her routine, not even her death from cancer six months ago.

"I believe you could fatten me up again," you offer, because there's nothing else for you to say. Whatever this is, whatever time you have left together, you'll let it belong to her.

It's the least you can do to repay the debt of love you owe her.

"I know it ain't much," she says, "but I can at least fix you a home-cooked meal. It's what I can do for you."

With that, she vanishes into the glare of the sunlight shining in through the open window.

"It's enough," you say, gazing at the empty place on the countertop where the tub of mussels seemed to rest only a moment ago. The pile of dirty rags you used to scrub the kitchen clean for the new owners is all that remains there now. "It should've always been enough."

Previous Publications

Acknowledgments

There are many people to acknowledge for both the existence of these stories and their safe passage into the world.

First, I want to thank all of those who've had a hand in making this book a reality, including my editor and publisher, Steve Berman; this book's fairy godfather and godmother, Michael Thomas Ford and Jennifer De Chiara; and most especially my cheerfully dauntless agent, Marie Lamba. I pulled a Royal Flush the day we met, Marie. Thank you for never saying no.

I also want to thank all the editors who have published my stories over the years, but especially Sheree Renée Thomas, Nora Shalaway Carpenter, and Sean Wallace. Your enthusiasm for my work came at a critical time in my career, and this book would not exist without your support.

My profound thanks to the dozens of writing teachers and mentors with whom I've had the good fortune to study. Specifically for this book I need to thank to

Elizabeth Partridge, who offered me the freedom and encouragement to try anything I wanted; and Helena Viramontes, whose generosity, kindness, and early faith in my work has been a loadstar. You told me this would happen all those years ago, Helena, and it finally has.

To the critique partners who've had a hand in making many of these stories better, thank you. This list includes (but is not limited to): Sarah Jefferis, Aimee Lehmann, Bob Proehl, Scott Brown, Bruce Need, Phil Tate, Shawn Goodman, Ted Blanchard, and Corey Farrenkopf.

Thanks to the WCYA community of the Vermont College of Fine Arts, and especially to my fellow Secret Gardeners. Thanks to Millay Arts for a magical and productive residency. Thank you to the amazing writers and volunteers of the Horror Writers Association. My eternal thanks and gratitude to the faculty, staff, and students of The Highlights Foundation for being my writing and teaching home away from home.

Special thanks to the circle of friends who have supported me and my writing over the years, especially Leslie Daniels, Alice Muhlback, Jill Swenson, Elizabeth Kuelbs, Jonathan Lenore Kastin, Laura Sibson, Mary Ellen Salmon, J.D. Gray, Paul McEuen, Susan Wiser, Anna Herforth, Martha Warren McKinney, and Elizabeth Braun Rush. Enormous thanks and endless love and admiration to my writing maven and fiercest champion, Nancy Werlin; to the big-hearted and sharp-witted, Melissa Wyatt; to the queen of play and peach sorbet, Sarah Aronson; to the wise and wondrous, Jennifer Richard Jacobson; to the brain-trusting, patriarchy-busting, kick-ass rockstar, Nicole Valentine; and to my dearest truth-teller, Anne Mazer.

Thank you to my parents, Victor and Karen Costello, and to my kind-hearted aunts, Judy Brockway and Lucille Costello. You've always supported me and my writing, no matter how weird it got. Dad, I wish you had lived long enough to see this.

Finally, to Werner Sun, my husband (and first and best reader): Words can never thank you enough. I love you with all I have in me.